Contents

Introduction

Why Traditional Tales?

And they all lived happily ever after...

Traditional tales are hundreds of years old, and yet they retain a special magic that is ready to be rediscovered by every generation of children. Their characters are memorable and larger-than-life, and their themes, which are never far below the surface, revolve around universal values and ideals.

Their storylines are distinctive and full of dramatic conflict. Yet those familiar words, "Once upon a time" (or their many variations) serve as a signal that all will turn out well: success will come to the good and the just; true love will triumph; wickedness will be punished; and hard work and kindness will be rewarded. Such storylines and clear outcomes create a level of predictability that is satisfying for all readers, especially younger ones — who particularly enjoy those stories where the smallest or youngest triumphs! The predictable story structures and outcomes invite children to become fully involved with the characters and their dilemmas, secure in the knowledge that "happily ever after" is never too far away.

Traditional tales have additional benefits for the classroom teacher. Each story provides an ideal starting point for exploring a diverse range of related activities, ensuring that the children's enjoyment doesn't end with the turning of the last page.

Appealing features

The stories in *Something Old, Something New* are firm favourites with children. As well as the characteristics already mentioned, they have features which make them all the more engaging and supportive for young readers:

- Inviting openings that quickly establish the setting and characters, and allow the reader to move rapidly into the story.

- Memorable language patterns and chants.

- Rhyme, repetition, alliteration and onomatopoeia.

- Recurring motifs, such as patterns of three.

In addition, readers enjoy becoming familiar with the typical forms of traditional tales: *Beast Tales*, such as *Puss-in-Boots; Wonder Tales*, such as *Jack and the Beanstalk; Pourquoi* (or *Why*) *Tales*, such as *Why Flies Buzz;* and *Cumulative Tales*, such as *Chicken Little.*

All of these story features provide models and inspiration for the children's own writing.

Once upon a time, a little red hen lived by herself in a house in the woods.

"Not I," quacked the duck.
"Not I," barked the dog.
"Not I," miaowed the cat.
"Not I," grunted the pig.

Wide-ranging appeal

Traditional tales appeal to children of all ages. How the stories are initially presented will depend on the children's reading experience and confidence, but each story has elements that appeal to all.

For example, young learners can readily enjoy the predictable storyline and rhythmic language of *The Three Billy Goats Gruff*, while older readers can consider the Troll's point of view and suggest how the problem could have been peacefully resolved.

This wide-ranging appeal is true of all stories featured in this book. In addition, the selection provides many opportunities for teachers to explore some sensitive issues; for example: *Chicken Little* (not following others blindly); *The Lion and the Mouse* (valuing individual talents); *The Ugly Duckling* (coping with rejection); *The Fisherman and His Wife* (greediness); *The Musicians of Bremen* (old age).

A further dimension can be added by encouraging children to read and compare different versions of the same story; a bibliography has been included to highlight some of these variations.

Traditional Tales in an Integrated Curriculum

Something Old, Something New reflects an integrated approach to traditional tales. It emphasizes the importance of engaging with the stories *as stories* and focusing on language, while at the same time showing the wide range of responses that can evolve from this experience. Depending on the book and the children, traditional tales can be ideal starting points for exploring aspects of mathematics, science, music, social studies, art and drama.

For each story there is a wide range of suggested activities, and teachers can decide which activities will be the most valuable for their students. One way of maximizing the use of this resource is to have groups of children working on different activities which can then be shared by all. Teachers can also adapt an activity suggested for one story in order to use it with another.

In addition, *Something Old, Something New* includes 17 Blackline Masters. Thirteen of these are designed to be used with specific stories; the remaining four can be used with any story.

The following is a small selection from the great wealth of learning experiences that traditional tales can provide:

Language activities

Language activities can involve a wide range of writing forms, from writing stories, letters and "how-to" instructions, to research and factual writing.

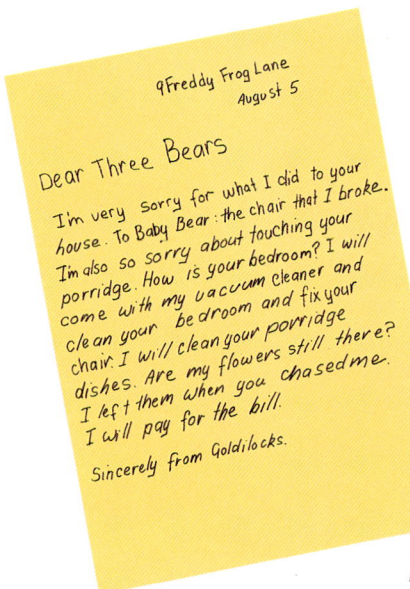

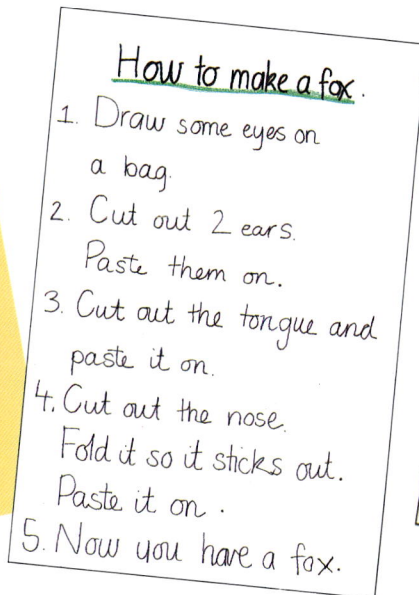

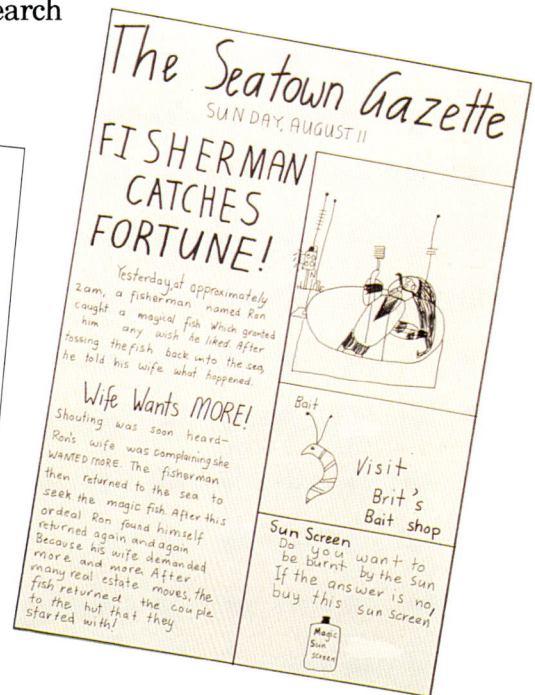

7

Mathematics

Traditional tales provide natural opportunities to explore mathematical concepts, from patterning and sequencing to number, measurement and graphing.

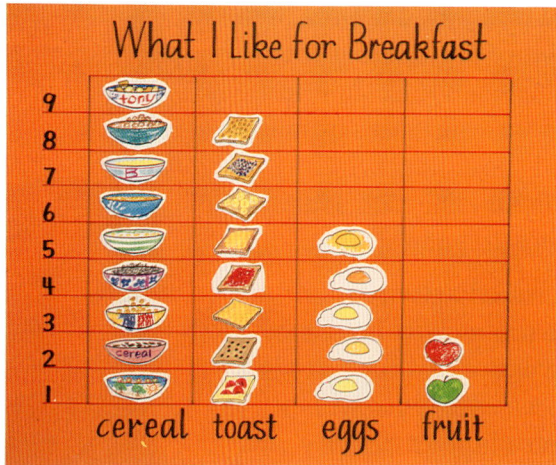

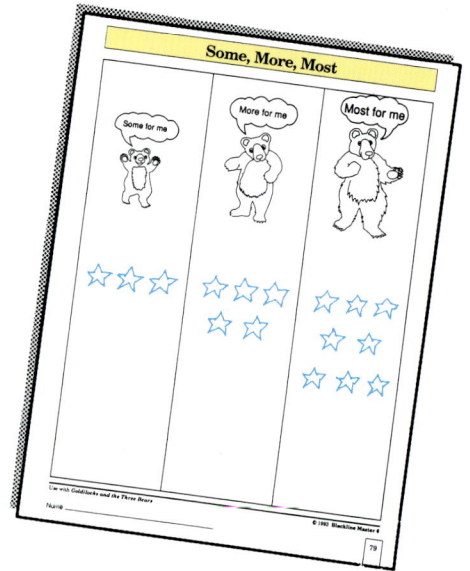

Science

Science activities, ranging from classification to observation and research, can be easily incorporated into the stories.

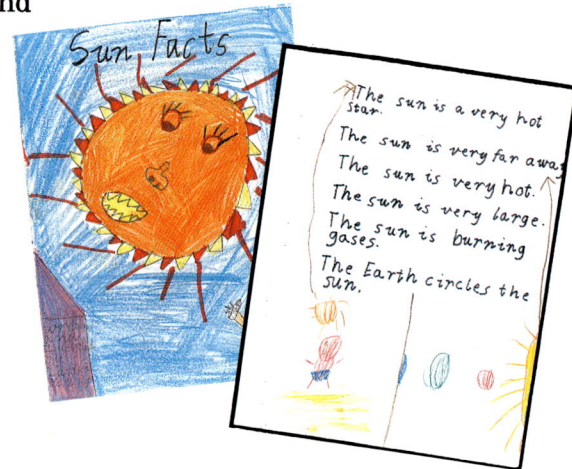

Social Studies

Social studies activities arise naturally from the stories — from talking about emotions to making maps and safety posters.

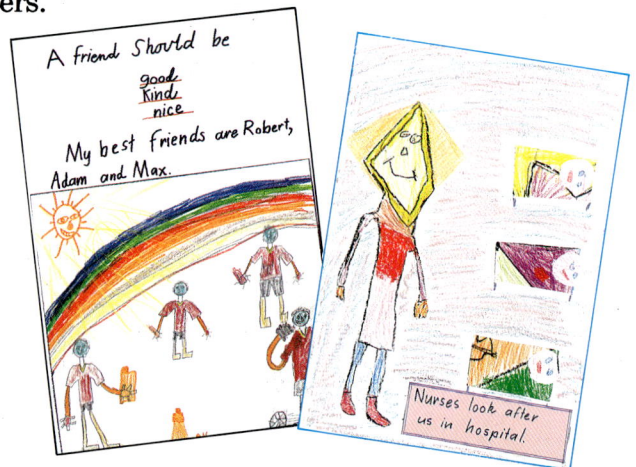

Art and Craft

Art is an integral part of the curriculum, providing many links to other subject areas, such as mathematics, drama, science and language.

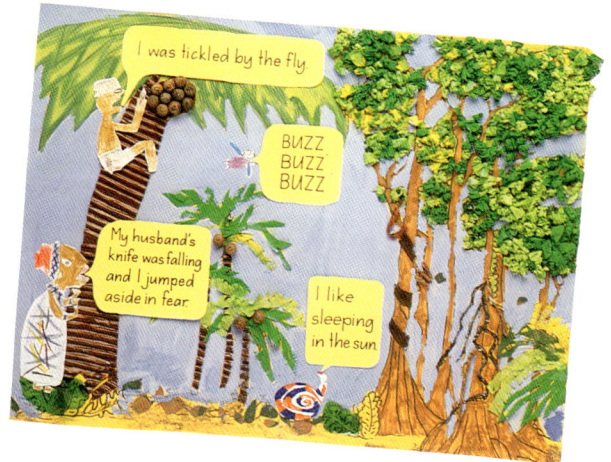

Drama

Music and drama provide many opportunities for making instruments, role plays, dialogue and acting out the story.

Something Old, Something New has been specifically designed to help teachers integrate traditional tales into their curriculum, allowing them to increase the children's enjoyment of the tales by extending the range of related classroom activities. It is a rich resource, full of suggestions and possibilities which, like the tales themselves, will be brought to life by the teachers and children who interpret them.

The Little Red Hen

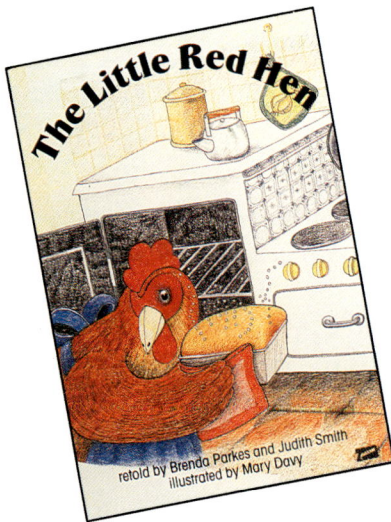

The Little Red Hen's predictable story structure and its simple theme — that laziness is punished and hard work rewarded — help to explain this story's perennial appeal to young readers. Its repetitive refrain of "Not I" makes it ideal for turn (or part) reading, and the process of wheat becoming bread leads naturally into a diverse range of related activities.

Throw the dice

Art and mathematics (counting)

- Discuss typical elements of board games, such as rules, penalty and bonus cards, starts and finishes.

- The children can design a *Little Red Hen* board game.

- Select events from the story which suit bonus and penalty cards. For example, *What if Little Red Hen lost the wheat?* (Penalty: go back 3 spaces!)

- Brainstorm the rules of the game, such as taking turns, and picking up cards. The children can write these rules in the order they will apply.

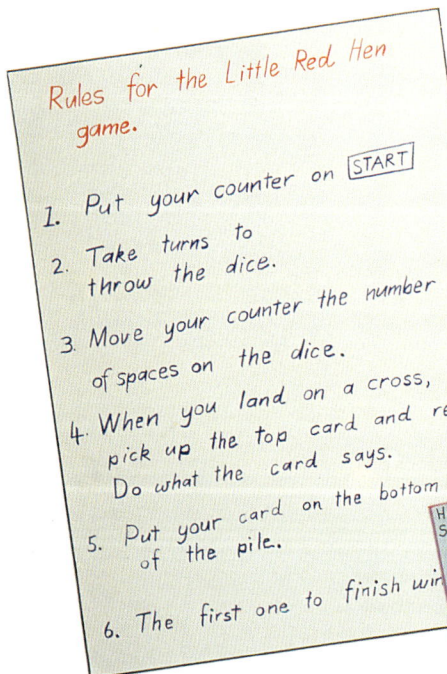

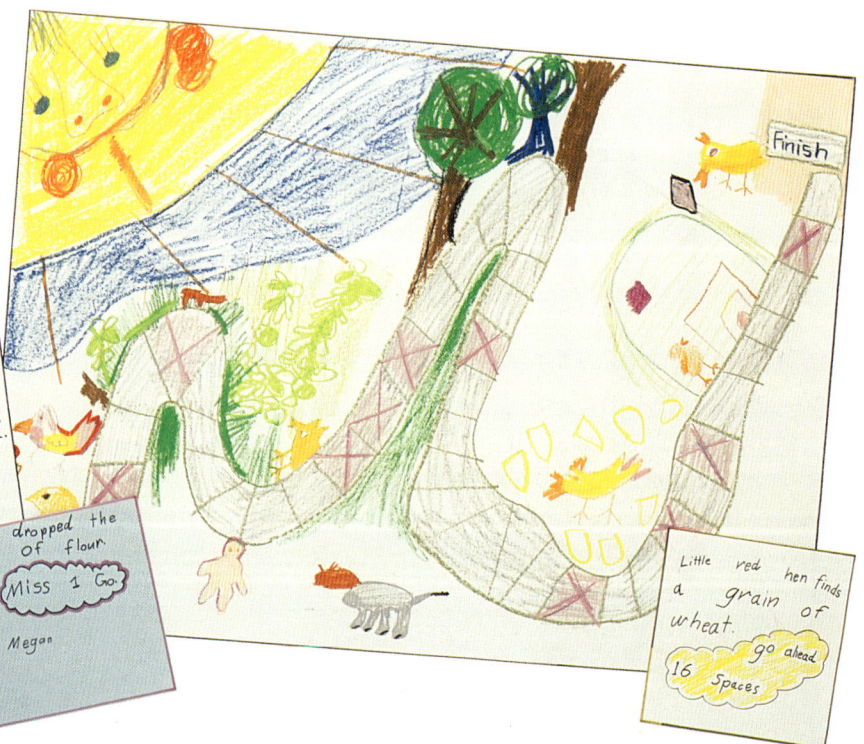

Rules for the Little Red Hen game.

1. Put your counter on START
2. Take turns to throw the dice.
3. Move your counter the number of spaces on the dice.
4. When you land on a cross, pick up the top card and read. Do what the card says.
5. Put your card on the bottom of the pile.
6. The first one to finish wir

Hen dropped the Sack of flour
Miss 1 Go.
Megan

Finish

Little red hen finds a grain of wheat. go ahead 16 spaces

Breakfast time

Health and science

- The children can do a class survey and record what they like eating for breakfast. Graph and discuss the results.

- *In the story, Little Red Hen eats fresh bread, but what do farm animals really eat?* Brainstorm some possibilities.

- Have the children select an animal and research its eating habits. They might explore questions such as, *Do animals need balanced diets? Do animals in the wild eat the same food as farm animals?*

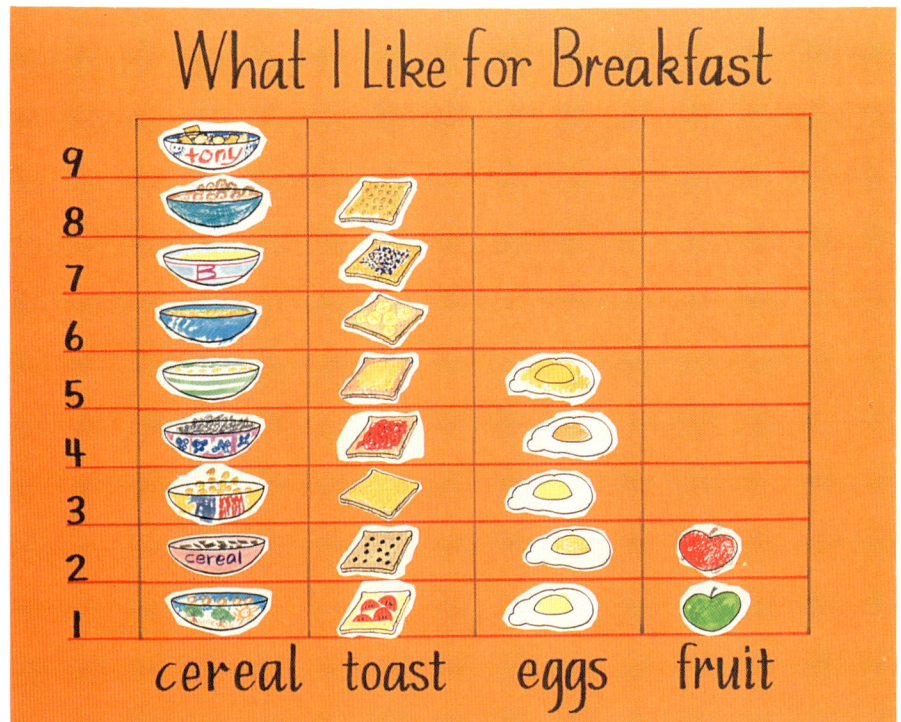

A friend should be . . .

Language and social studies

- Discuss the qualities found in a good friend; list these on the board.

- The children can write a heading such as, *A friend should be*, and then list three of the qualities they value in a friend. They can then name a friend and illustrate the poster.

- Discuss the way the other animals behaved towards Little Red Hen. *Were they very friendly? Did their attitudes change? Why?*

- As a follow-up, the children can write letters to the other animals in the story, explaining why Little Red Hen didn't want to share her bread with them.

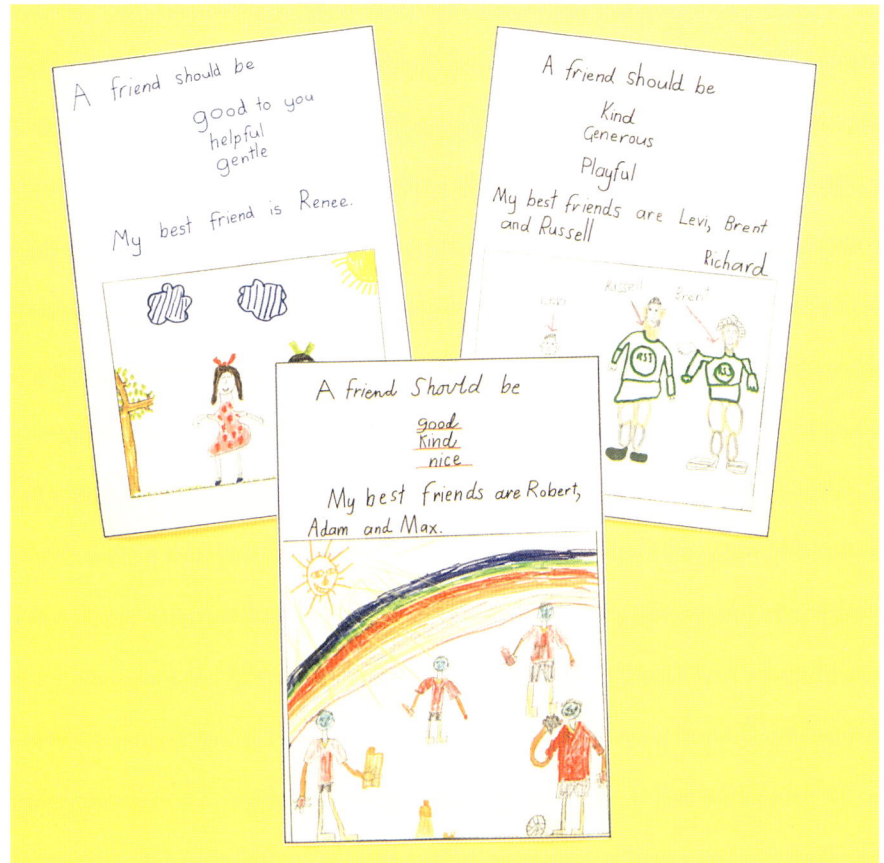

The chicken and the egg

Science (investigating life cycles)

- The children can investigate questions about hens. For example, *What are baby hens called? How long does it take for a chicken to hatch? When do chickens start to lay eggs? How long do hens live for?*

- Have the children explore different ways of showing this information as a timeline or as a life cycle chart.

- To follow up, the children can investigate other animals and birds that hatch from eggs.

Hens sit on their nests for 21 days before the eggs hatch.

Life Cycle of a hen.

A busy hen

Compiling lists, sequencing

- Discuss the work Little Red Hen does on the farm.

- Have the children work in pairs to list Little Red Hen's chores in the order in which she carries them out.

- As a follow-up, discuss and list other things that we do in a sequence of steps, such as getting ready for school, or making a sandwich.

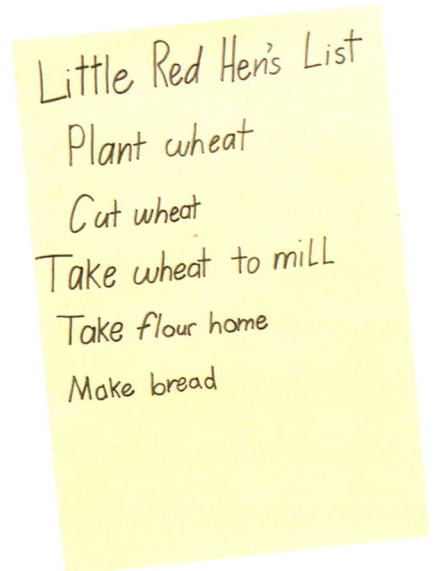

Little Red Hen's List
Plant wheat
Cut wheat
Take wheat to mill
Take flour home
Make bread

Farm animals

Language (factual writing)

- Brainstorm a list of the animals on Little Red Hen's farm.

- The children can select an animal and work in groups to find out more about it, such as its size, appearance, eating habits, the sound it makes and what its babies are called.

- The children can write and illustrate this information. Display the work as posters, or compile into a book.

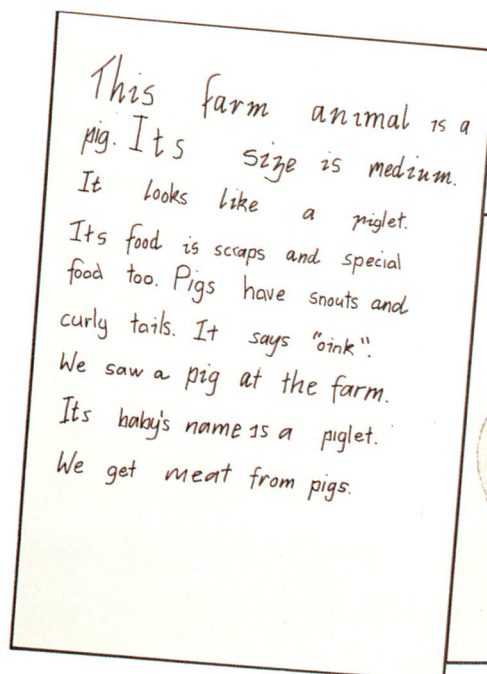

This farm animal is a pig. Its size is medium. It looks like a piglet. Its food is scraps and special food too. Pigs have snouts and curly tails. It says "oink". We saw a pig at the farm. Its baby's name is a piglet. We get meat from pigs.

Everybody helps

Language and social studies

- Brainstorm a list of occupations.
- Ask the children what those jobs involve; for example, *How do dentists help us?*
- The children can then select an occupation and write about it.
- Discuss and list chores that the children perform at home.
- The children can select one of these chores, then describe and illustrate it.
- Display the children's posters under a heading such as, *How I help at home.*

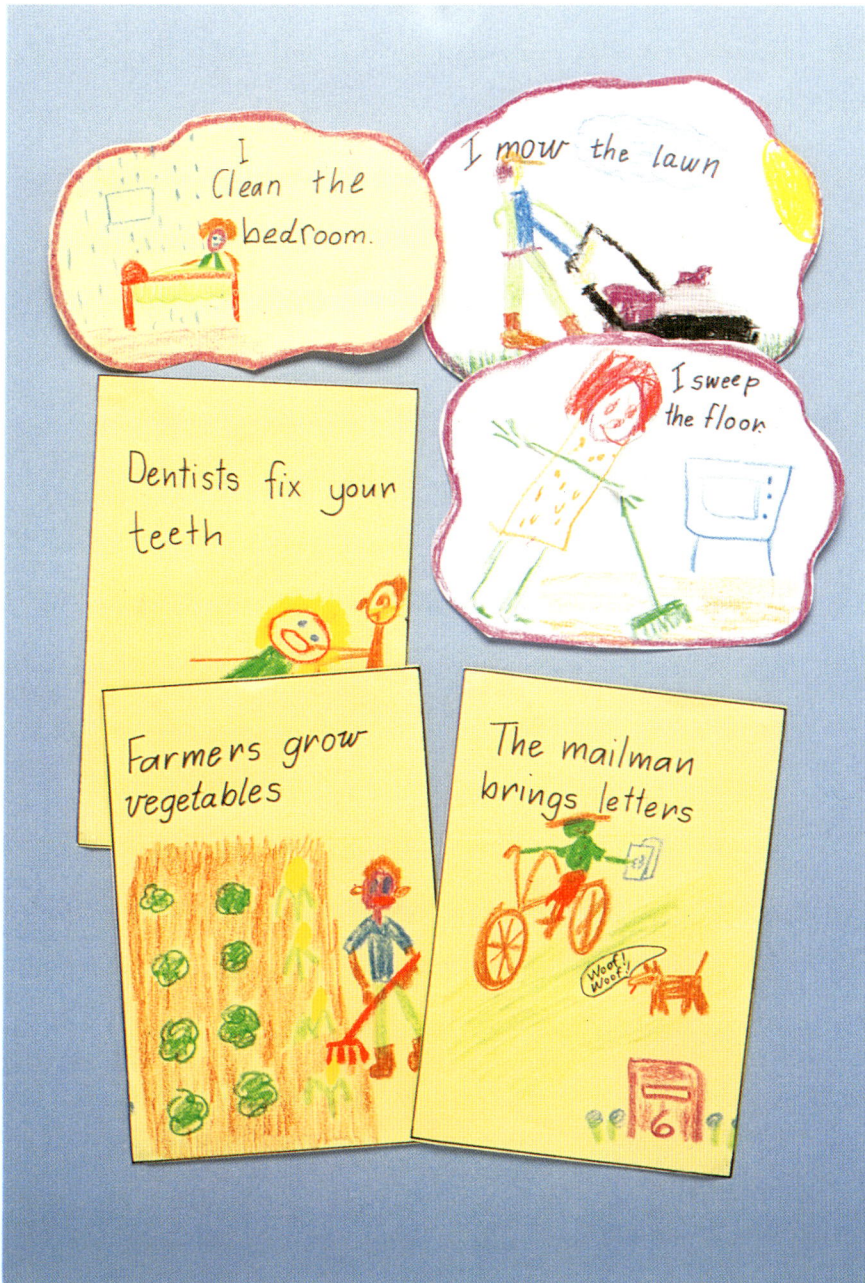

What comes next?

Exploring plot

- Give each child a copy of Blackline Master 1 and Blackline Master 2.
- The children can cut out both shapes along the dotted lines.
- The children can select five events from the story and draw them in sequence on Blackline Master 2.
- They can then join both wheels with a butterfly pin so the drawings are seen one by one.
- Compare the children's story wheels. *Which events did you choose? Why?*
- The children can use their story wheels to retell the story for one another.

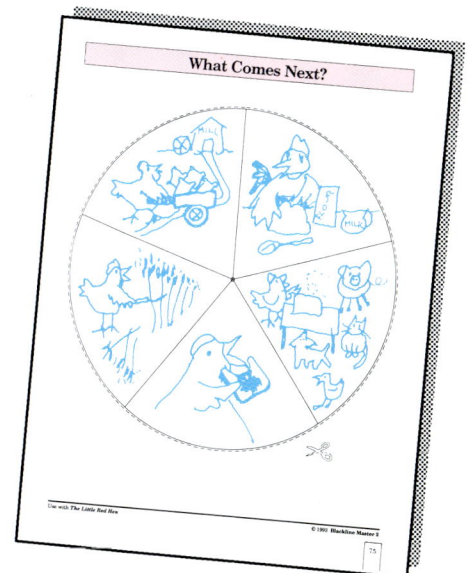

The Gingerbread Man

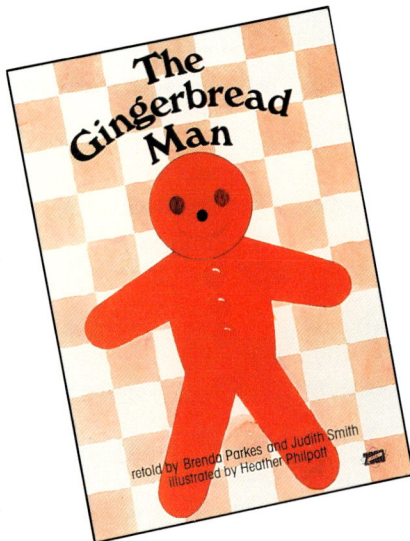

The Gingerbread Man is one of the most well known traditional stories. Its cumulative structure and memorable refrain combine to make a story that is highly engaging and predictable. The strongly patterned text provides a ready model for innovation, and an ideal starting point for integrated curriculum activities.

Exploring character

Descriptive writing

- Reread the story to the class. Ask the children to listen for clues about the Gingerbread Man's ingredients, what he might taste like, and what happens to him in the story.

- Discuss how information about the Gingerbread Man could be compiled. Below are some of the possibilities:
  — Make an information web.
  — List statements about the Gingerbread Man, and underline key words.
  — Have the children write descriptive paragraphs about the Gingerbread Man.

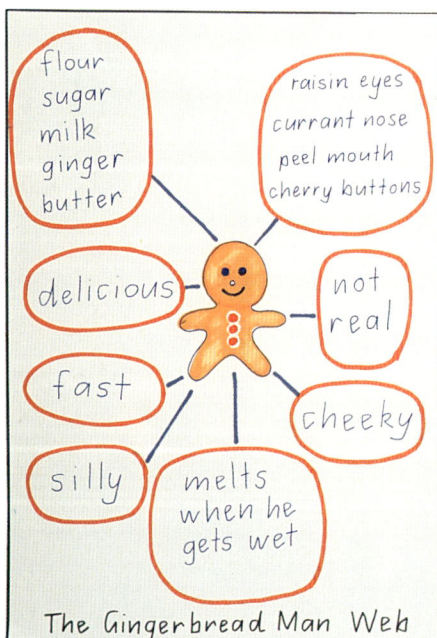

flour
sugar
milk
ginger
butter

raisin eyes
currant nose
peel mouth
cherry buttons

delicious

not real

fast

cheeky

silly

melts when he gets wet

The Gingerbread Man Web

What we know about the Gingerbread Man.

1. He is <u>delicious</u>.
2. He is made of <u>ginger</u>, <u>flour</u>, <u>milk</u>, <u>butter</u> and <u>sugar</u>.
3. He is <u>decorated</u> with <u>raisin</u> eyes, <u>currant</u> nose, <u>peel</u> mouth and <u>cherry</u> buttons.
4. He runs very <u>fast</u>.
5. He is a bit <u>silly</u>.
6. He is very <u>cheeky</u>.
7. He is <u>not real</u>.
8. If he gets wet, he will <u>melt</u>

The Gingerbread man

He is made of ginger, flour, milk, butter and Sugar. He runs very fast. He's delicious. He has raisin eyes, currant nose, Cherry buttons, peel mouth. He will melt if he goes in Water. He's silly and he's cheeky.

by Michael

Making gingerbread men

Following and writing recipes

- Collect simple gingerbread recipes to share and compare. *What features do they have in common? Do they use the same utensils and ingredients as those used in the book?*

- Select a recipe to follow to make gingerbread men with the children.

- Afterwards, the children can write "how-to" instructions telling about the steps they followed.

- (Note: If it is difficult to arrange real cooking with the class, use the recipe on Blackline Master 17 to make model gingerbread men.)

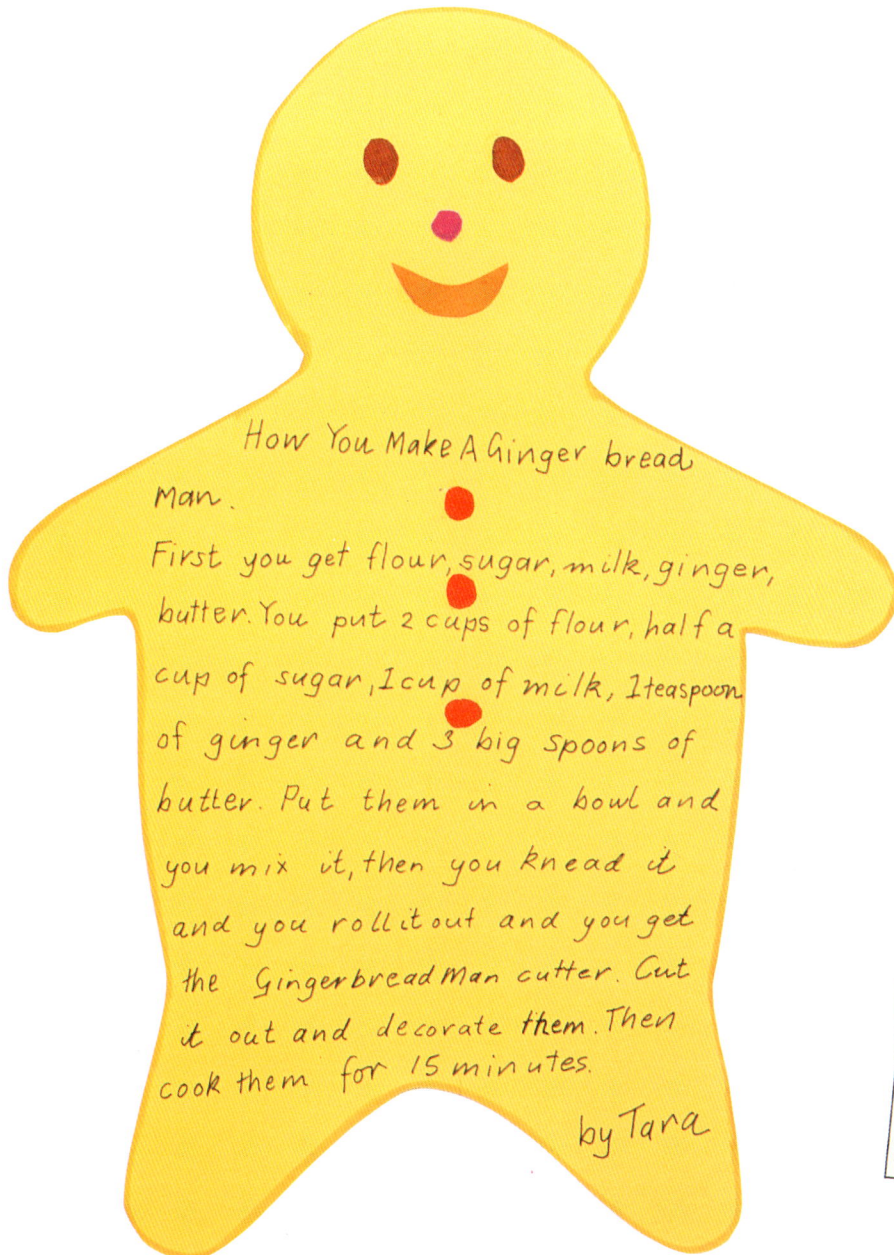

How You Make A Ginger bread Man.

First you get flour, sugar, milk, ginger, butter. You put 2 cups of flour, half a cup of sugar, 1 cup of milk, 1 teaspoon of ginger and 3 big spoons of butter. Put them in a bowl and you mix it, then you knead it and you roll it out and you get the Gingerbread Man cutter. Cut it out and decorate them. Then cook them for 15 minutes.

by Tara

Where food comes from

Health and social studies

- The children can work in groups researching one of the ingredients used to make gingerbread.

- They can make charts to show how the ingredient changes from raw material to finished product.

- The children can collect food wrappers from products which include the ingredients they have researched. Discuss these foods in terms of nutritional value and balanced diets.

- As a follow-up activity, find out where the ingredients in gingerbread might have been grown. Pin wool on a map to show the route they might have taken to get to your town.

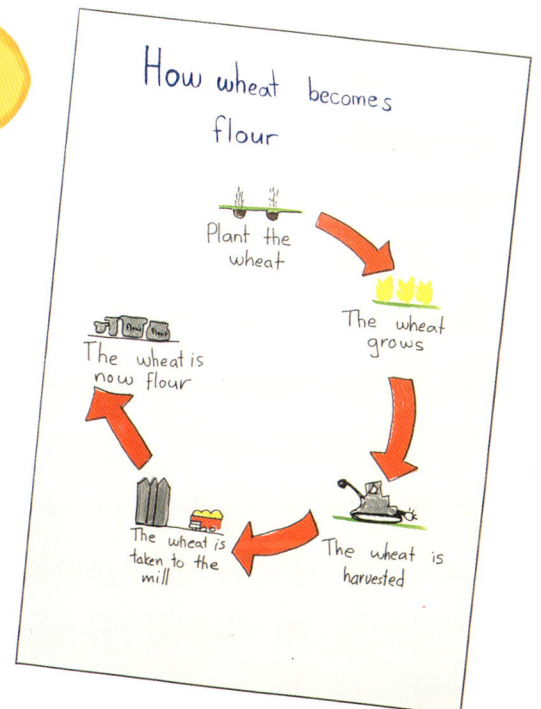

How wheat becomes flour

Plant the wheat

The wheat grows

The wheat is harvested

The wheat is taken to the mill

The wheat is now flour

Changing perspective

Exploring point of view

- Have the children consider the story from the fox's or the old man's point of view.
- Ask questions relating to a character's feelings, such as, *How did the old man feel when the Gingerbread Man ran away?*

- The children can select a character and write his or her version of the story.
- As a follow-up activity, the children can mime or act out one character's point of view.

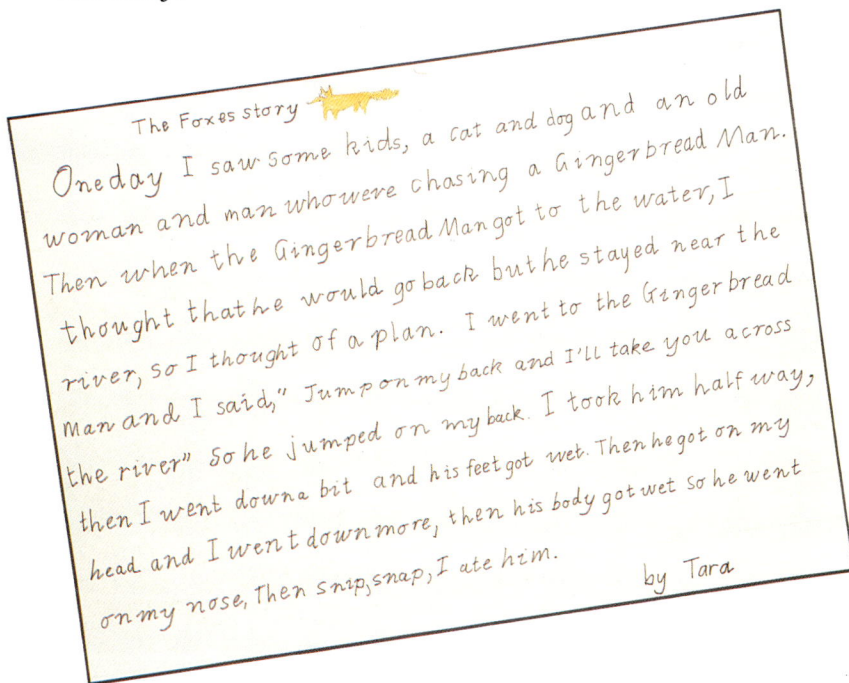

The Foxes story

One day I saw some kids, a cat and dog and an old woman and man who were chasing a Gingerbread Man. Then when the Gingerbread Man got to the water, I thought that he would go back but he stayed near the river, so I thought of a plan. I went to the Gingerbread Man and I said," Jump on my back and I'll take you across the river" So he jumped on my back. I took him half way, then I went down a bit and his feet got wet. Then he got on my head and I went down more, then his body got wet so he went on my nose, Then snip, snap, I ate him.

by Tara

Missing person

Stating the essentials

- Discuss the language of Missing Persons posters (brief, factual), and the details they normally include: description, locality, appearance, reward.
- The children can write and illustrate their own Missing Persons posters. Share and display.

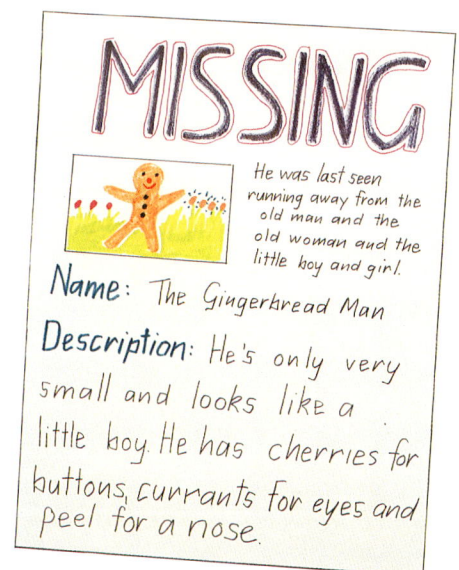

MISSING

He was last seen running away from the old man and the old woman and the little boy and girl.

Name: The Gingerbread Man

Description: He's only very small and looks like a little boy. He has cherries for buttons, currants for eyes and peel for a nose.

Making a collage

Exploring textures and patterns

- Collect a variety of fabric scraps.
- Discuss which fabrics suit which character, and why.
- The children can select an event, illustrate it with a collage, and write a caption.
- Alternatively, cut shapes from paper painted with patterns of the children's choice.

The Gingerbread Man ran past a dog and a cat. "STOP!" cried the dog. "STOP!" cried the cat. But the Gingerbread Man ran faster and faster.

Creating a chant

Exploring rhyme and rhythm

- Use the Gingerbread Man's refrain of *Run, run as fast as you can* as a springboard for exploring rhyme and rhythm.

- Brainstorm a list of action words that could be used in chants; for example, *hop, leap* and *jump*.

- Have the children select a character from the story and write a chant for him or her.

- The children can create music for their chants; this might include making their own musical instruments.

- Have the children perform their chants for the class.

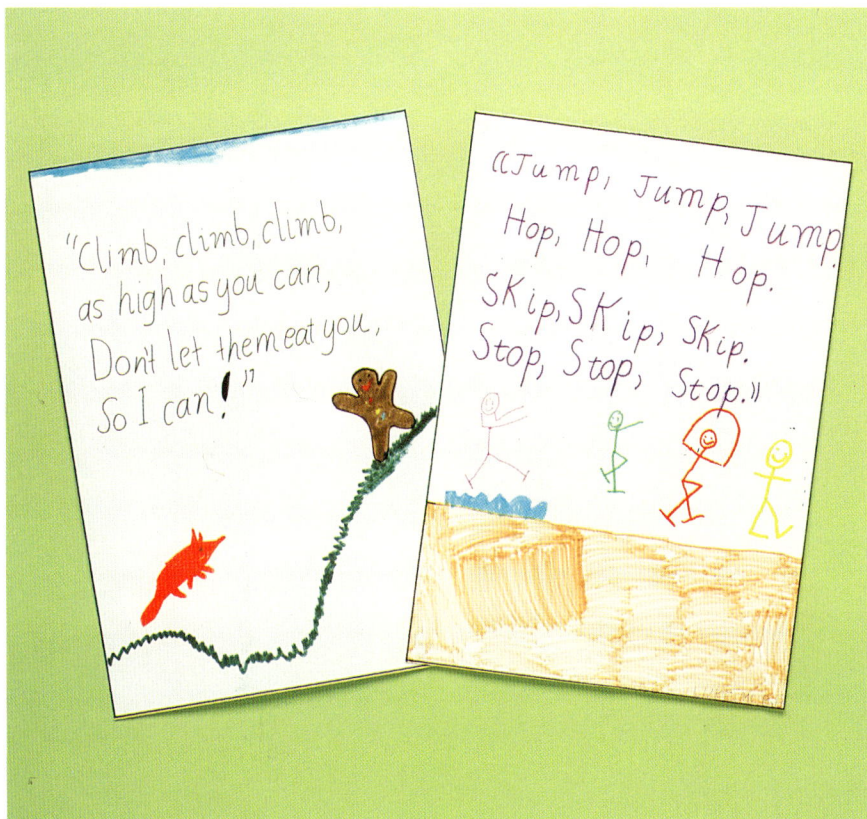

Then what happened?

Extending the plot, problem solving

- Discuss alternative endings to the story; for example, the Gingerbread Man might climb a tree, or the old man might catch him.

- Each child can then complete a copy of Blackline Master 3 to show a new ending.

- Share and discuss the children's different solutions.

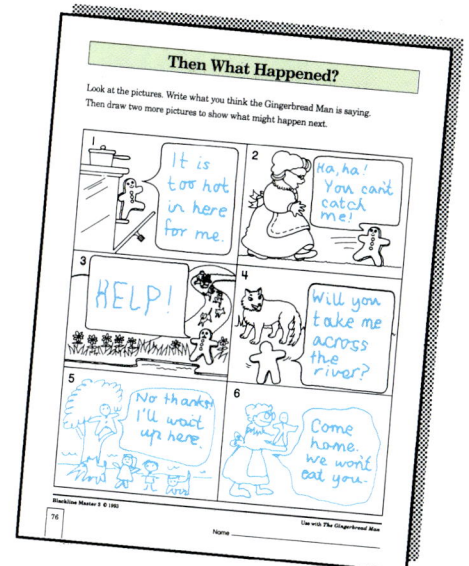

Other suggestions

- Act out the story using finger puppets cut from old gloves.
- Set up an activity centre for weighing and measuring.
- Use paint and kitchen utensils such as potato mashers, forks and spatulas to make kitchen prints.
- Compare different versions of the story; how do they differ?

The Fox and the Little Red Hen

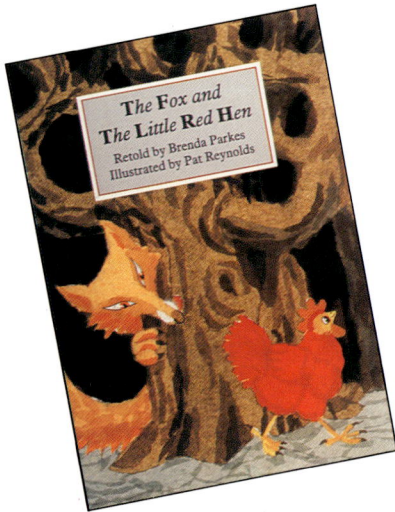

The Fox and the Little Red Hen is an engaging and strongly patterned story which encourages a high level of reader participation. In addition, the story is a good model for children's writing and invites responses in areas such as art, science and language.

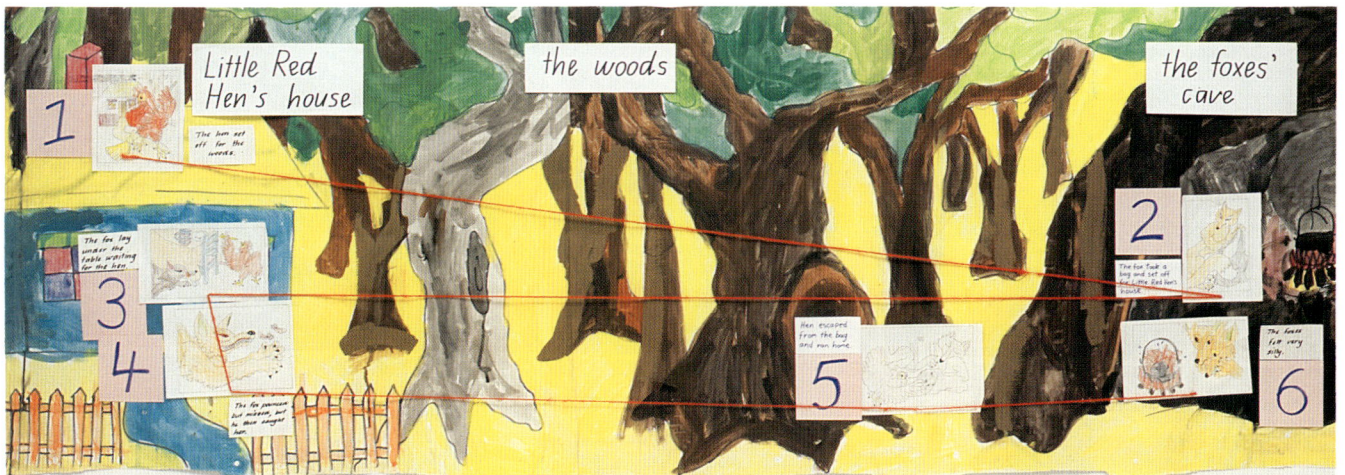

A mural story map

Exploring story structure

- Discuss the main locations of the story. The children can work in groups to illustrate these. Combine the pictures to form a mural.

- As you reread the story, the children can use wool to map the main events on the mural. For example, the story starts at the hen's house, then goes to the foxes' cave, and then back to the house.

- Later, you might write the main events on separate cards. The children can attach these to the mural as they retell the story.

That's just like . . .

Matching and comparing

- Compare *The Fox and the Little Red Hen* with the story of *The Little Red Hen*.
- Help the children to write statements about the stories on separate cards, such as what the hens eat, and how they are illustrated in the books.
- The children can then take turns finding "pairs" of cards and placing them next to each other on a chart.

The Fox and the Little Red Hen

- the Little Red Hen lives on her own in a house
- the Little Red Hen scratches for food
- the foxes talk, but the Little Red Hen just squawks
- the Little Red Hen has a yellow beak
- the Little Red Hen was collage
- the picture on the cover goes over onto the back of the book

The Little Red Hen

- the Little Red Hen lives with other animals
- the Little Red Hen cooks her food
- the Little Red Hen talks
- the Little Red Hen has a white beak
- the Little Red Hen was drawn and painted
- the cover picture is only on the front

Both of the stories end happily for the Little Red Hens

Character mobile

Exploring character

- Write words from the book's title on pieces of thin card. Suspend pictures of the fox and the hen from them.
- Brainstorm ideas about what the characters were like and what they did.
- Write the information on cards and display as a mobile.

The Fox — and

The Little Red Hen

The fox lived on the other side of the wood.

The fox missed when he pounced on the hen.

The hen lived on one side of the wood.

The fox watches the hen, planning to catch her.

The hen scratches in the wood for food.

The foxes felt silly when they were tricked.

Designing a house

Visual thinking

- Review the story, looking for clues about Little Red Hen's house; for example, it is described as being near woods and having rafters, and some of its furniture is depicted.

- Brainstorm any special features a hen's house might need, such as an egg-laying room.

- The children can design a house for Little Red Hen. This could be a floor plan or a model. Share and display.

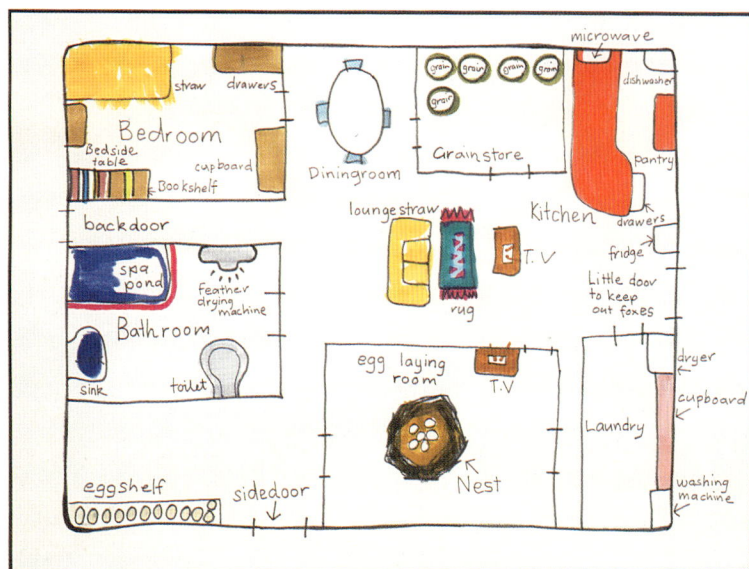

A new leaf

Science (sorting and classifying)

- Go on a leaf hunt around the school or in a nearby park. Collect assorted leaves and bring them back to the classroom.

- The children can decide how to group the leaves; possibilities include sorting by shape, colour, texture, width, symmetry or vein patterns.

- They can then make charts showing their different leaf groupings. Share and display.

All about foxes

Science (animal behaviour)

- The children can investigate foxes; for example, where they originated, where they are found today, people's attitudes towards them, what their babies are called, if they live alone or in groups, and what they like to eat.

- The children can record and illustrate the information they discover. The pages can be displayed as posters or put together to form a big book.

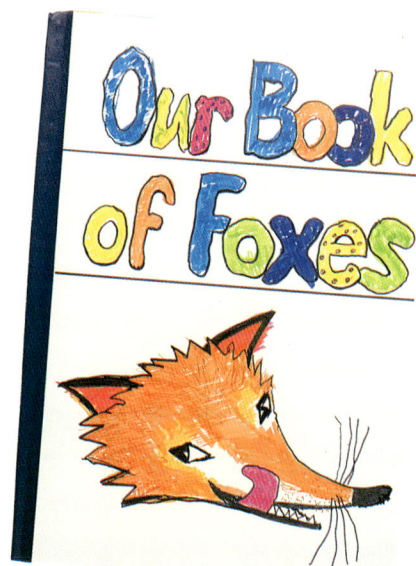

Making fox and hen puppets

Art and language

- Collect glue, scissors, crayons, scraps of coloured paper, and a paper bag for each child,

- The children can draw eyes on the bag and decide on appropriate shapes for each character's features. These features can be cut out and pasted to the paper bags.

- Use the puppets to act out the story as it is narrated.

- To follow up, the children can write instructions to help a friend make a fox or a hen.

How to make a fox.

1. Draw some eyes on a bag
2. Cut out 2 ears. Paste them on.
3. Cut out the tongue and paste it on.
4. Cut out the nose. Fold it so it sticks out. Paste it on.
5. Now you have a fox

Fox and hen hand puppets add an extra dimension to retellings of the story.

Filling the gaps

Reading for meaning

- Write out the story on large sheets of paper, omitting selected words. The children can work in pairs to fill in the gaps and illustrate the page.

- Share the words the children have used. Then put the pages together to form a book.

When Fox came to Little _Red_ Hen's house, she was _out_ in the woods scratching for _food_.

Tammy. Belinda

She rolled a big _stone_ into a bag. Then she ran home as fast _as_ she could.

The Three Little Pigs

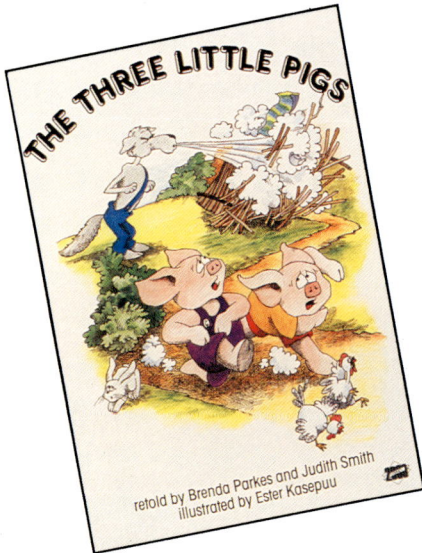

The Three Little Pigs combines a strong storyline with several classic elements of traditional tales: patterns of three; a cast of wicked, foolish and brave characters; and the theme of cleverness overcoming force. This story lends itself to a range of responses in drama, art and mathematics.

Making the wolf and pigs

Art and mathematics (sorting and measurement)

- Collect assorted fabric scraps.

- Discuss ideas for making the wolf and the pigs. *What size and shape will they be?* Collect large cardboard pieces and cut out the agreed-upon shapes.

- Discuss clothing for each character; the children can then sort the fabric scraps and paste them onto the shapes.

- Discuss ways of describing the characters; for example, using measurement ideas.

Building houses

Art and mathematics (creating patterns)

- Discuss the materials the pigs used to build their houses.
- The children can cut out house shapes from cardboard and decorate them with straws, craft sticks and "bricks" (painted paper rectangles).
- Encourage the children to create patterns as they arrange the materials.
- Discuss the houses and then use them as props for drama and retellings.

Making sock puppets

Art and drama

- The children can bring puppet-making materials from home: socks, buttons, aerosol can lids and scraps of felt and fabric.
- *To make a pig:* Put an aerosol can lid into the toe of a sock and tie with a rubber band. Add buttons for eyes, and felt shapes for nostrils, ears and tongue.
- *To make a wolf:* Crumple paper into a sock and tie to form a nose; add felt rectangles for ears and buttons for eyes.

Now that you have the wolf, the pigs and the houses, it's time to put on a play!

Finding the way

Mapping and giving directions

- Brainstorm ideas for drawing maps based on the story. *What features should be included? Who might find the map helpful?*

- The children can work in pairs to draw their maps.

- As a follow-up, the children can map aspects of their own environment; for example, a letter inviting friends home to play might include a map to show them the way.

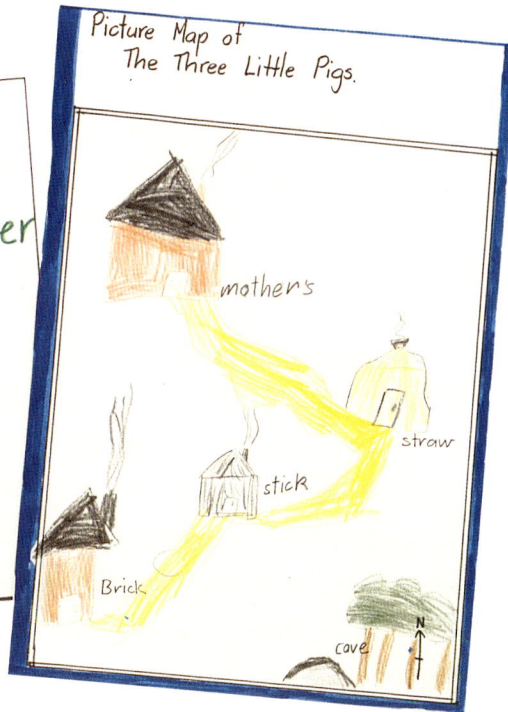

Will you come to my house after school to Play?

Picture Map of The Three Little Pigs.

mother's

straw

stick

Brick

cave

N

Catch that pig!

Problem solving

- Discuss the wolf's attempts to catch the pigs. *Was he successful? What else could he have done?* Brainstorm other methods the wolf might have tried, such as digging a tunnel under the houses or dropping a net on the pigs.

- Give the children copies of Blackline Master 4 and have them devise pig-catching plans of their own. Share and display the plans.

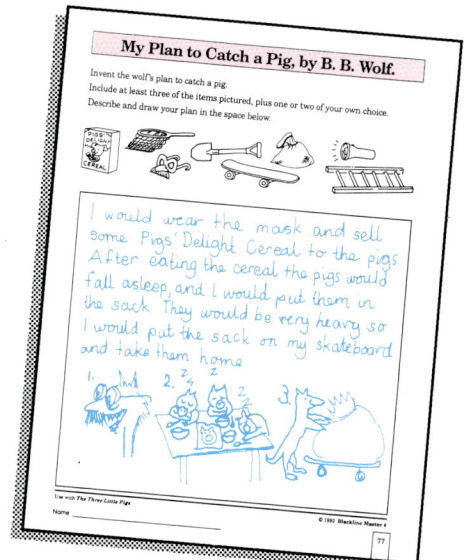

My Plan to Catch a Pig, by B. B. Wolf.

Invent the wolf's plan to catch a pig.
Include at least three of the items pictured, plus one or two of your own choice.
Describe and draw your plan in the space below.

I would wear the mask and sell some Pigs' Delight Cereal to the pigs. After eating the cereal the pigs would fall asleep, and I would put them in the sack. They would be very heavy so I would put the sack on my skateboard and take them home.

Use with *The Three Little Pigs*

Name

77

The Wolf's diary

Language (point of view)

- Review the order of events.

- Discuss diaries and the way they are written: the use of first person ("I" not "the wolf"), and the recording of dates and feelings.

- Rewrite the story as a series of entries from the wolf's diary.

<u>Monday</u>
Saw three fat pigs walking through woods. Watched the smallest one make a house out of straw. Ha, Ha, Ha. What a dumb thing to do.

<u>Tuesday</u>
Little pig has finished his straw house. He thinks he's safe. Ha, Ha, Ha. He's not safe from the big bad wolf! The middle pig is building a stick house.

<u>Wednesday</u>
Huffed and puffed and blew down the straw house and the stick house. Fat little pigs are in the brick house with their smart brother. Tomorrow I'll climb down the chimney and eat all of them. Ha, Ha, Ha.

What is it?

Science (classifying materials)

- Collect objects that have different textures, such as wood, leaves, soap, felt, sandpaper, pebbles and wool.

- Cut a hole in a box and put the objects inside. The children can take turns reaching into the box and trying to identify an object by feel.

- The children can now decide how to group the objects; for example, hard, soft, smooth or rough. *Is every object in a group? Are any objects in more than one group?*

- To follow up, the children can write statements and questions about texture and touch, for future discussion and research.

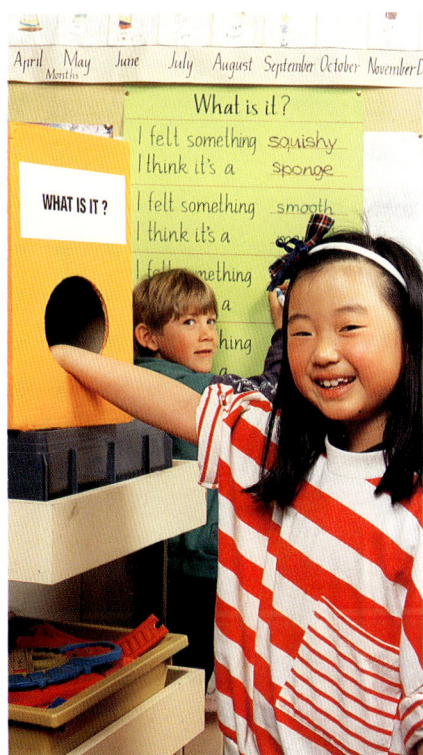

How did they feel?

Using language to describe emotions

- Brainstorm words to describe each character's feelings. Ask questions such as, *How did the Mother Pig feel when the three little pigs left home? How did the first pig feel when his house was blown down? How did he feel when he reached the wooden house?*

- List "feeling" words for each character.

- The children can use these words in their own stories.

Other suggestions

- The children can write their own "three" stories; for example, The Three Dragons or The Three Sheep.

- The children can use cotton buds as brushes to paint portraits of the pigs.

- Create a landscape collage for a backdrop, then perform *The Three Little Pigs* as a play.

25

Goldilocks and the Three Bears

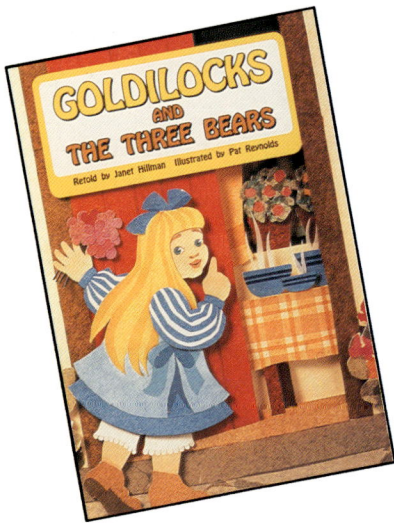

Goldilocks and the Three Bears is one of the best-loved of all traditional stories, with a repetitive pattern that makes joining in irresistible. The ideas of number and comparison embedded in the story provide a natural integration of language and mathematics, and reader response activities can easily be adapted to provide different levels of challenge.

Goldilocks says "sorry"

Exploring character through letter writing

- Collect samples of letters. *What features do they have in common?*

- Brainstorm letters that could arise from this story, such as an apology from Goldilocks or a letter of complaint.

- The children can work in pairs to write and edit their letters.

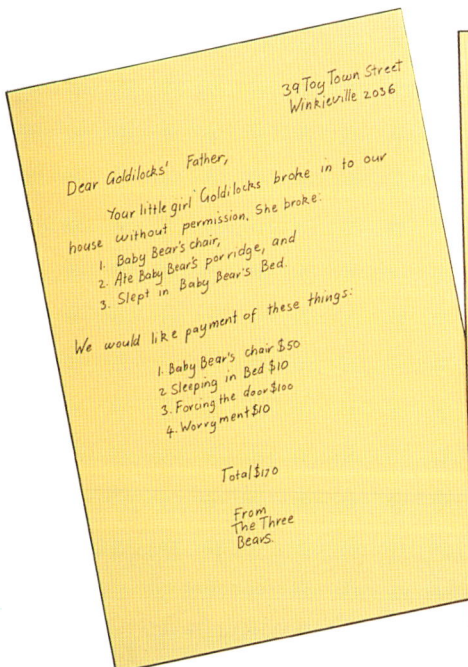

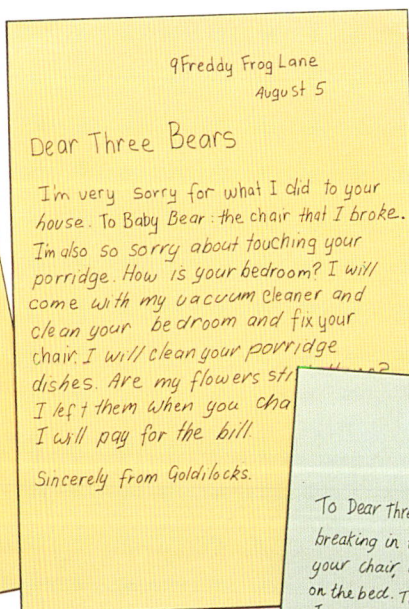

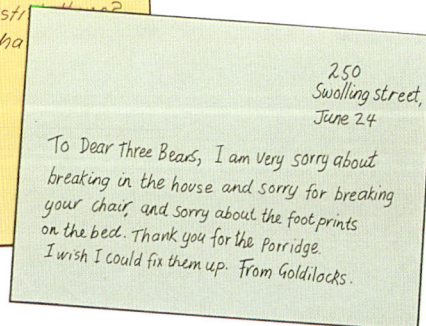

- Share and display.

39 Toy Town Street
Winkieville 2036

Dear Goldilocks' Father,

Your little girl Goldilocks broke in to our house without permission. She broke:
1. Baby Bear's chair,
2. Ate Baby Bear's porridge, and
3. Slept in Baby Bear's Bed.

We would like payment of these things:
1. Baby Bear's chair $50
2. Sleeping in Bed $10
3. Forcing the door $100
4. Worrygment $10

Total $170

From
The Three Bears.

9 Freddy Frog Lane
August 5

Dear Three Bears

I'm very sorry for what I did to your house. To Baby Bear: the chair that I broke. I'm also so sorry about touching your porridge. How is your bedroom? I will come with my vacuum cleaner and clean your bedroom and fix your chair. I will clean your porridge dishes. Are my flowers sti.... I left them when you cha.... I will pay for the bill.

Sincerely from Goldilocks.

250
Swolling street,
June 24

To Dear Three Bears, I am very sorry about breaking in the house and sorry for breaking your chair, and sorry about the footprints on the bed. Thank you for the porridge. I wish I could fix them up. From Goldilocks.

Furnishing the three bears' house

Mathematics (sorting and classifying)

- Collect advertising materials which show a wide range of furniture. Collect wallpaper scraps and cut them into house shapes — one for each child.

- Using the pictures in *Goldilocks* as a starting point, discuss appropriate furnishings for the different rooms of a house.

- Have the children select a room; they can then choose and paste pictures to match that room.

- Discuss and display.

Wanted poster

Art and language (factual writing)

- Bring in some examples of Lost and Found notices. Discuss the type of language and information they contain (brief, factual).

- Working in pairs, the children can write Wanted or Lost notices for each other.

- Share some examples. *Can you identify which classmate is on the poster?*

- The children can then create Wanted posters for Goldilocks.

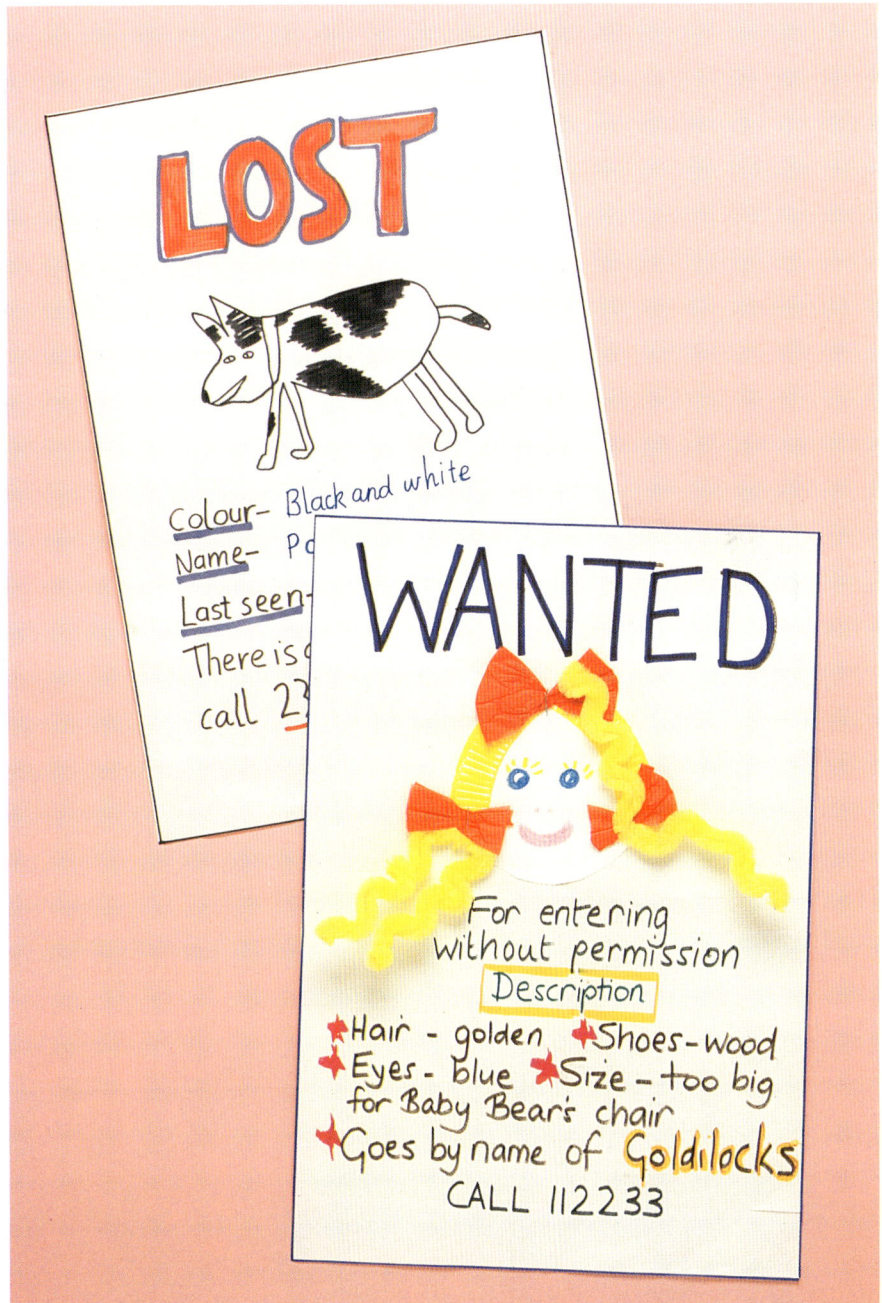

- Share and display.

Pa and Mama bear's bed room

Baby Bear's bed room

LOST

Colour- Black and white
Name- P...
Last seen-
There is...
call 23...

WANTED

For entering without permission
Description
★ Hair - golden ★ Shoes - wood
★ Eyes - blue ★ Size - too big
for Baby Bear's chair
★ Goes by name of Goldilocks
CALL 112233

Write your own thought bubbles

Matching and inferencing

- After rereading the story, give the children copies of Blackline Master 5; have them look through the story and find the pages that match each of the pictures.

- Taking each picture in turn, the children can add that character's thoughts to the speech bubble.

- Have the children share their writing; discuss different interpretations of the same event.

Torn paper collage

Art

- Collect paper scraps of varying texture and colour.

- As a class, discuss the way that *Goldilocks* is illustrated.

- Have the children illustrate scenes from the story using cut or torn paper.

A scroll story

Language (sequencing and retelling)

- List the story's main events; the children can select an event and work in pairs to write about and illustrate it.

- Sequence the events and tape them into a scroll.

- Cut a slot into a box and insert one end of the scroll.

- Tape the other end of the scroll to a cardboard tube and attach to the box with twisties. Use the scroll for retelling the story.

Some, more, most

Mathematics (quantity and comparison)

- Give each child a copy of Blackline Master 6.

- Use the story as a starting point to explore comparisons of quantity. The children can use the Blackline Master to act out these comparisons. For example: *Baby Bear has three raisins. How many raisins could you give to Mama Bear so that she has more? How many raisins for Papa Bear?*

Other breakfasts

Matching and comparing

- Discuss characters in other stories. *What might they eat for breakfast?* The children can suggest foods and quantities for specific characters.

- The children can work in pairs to select a character and create a breakfast menu.

- Share and display.

Making bears' ears

Measurement and art

- Provide strips and circles of heavy-weight paper. Have the children use the strips to measure each other's heads; they can then use them to make headbands.

- Attach the circles to the headbands to form bears' ears.

- Use the bears' ears as props to act out the story.

29

The Lion and the Mouse

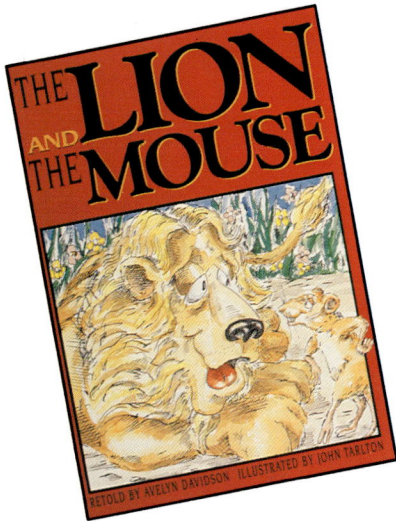

The Lion and the Mouse is a simple yet powerful fable that is always popular with young readers. Its strong, cumulative plot — in which small, clever Mouse rescues big, helpless Lion — and clever use of rhyme, rhythm and repetition, combine to make a story that is both appealing and easy to read.

Investigating word shapes

Art and language

- Reread the story. *Why might the lion's speech be in large bold letters?* Find other ways of expressing the meaning of a word by its shape, such as

Little Mouse ran o^v^{e}r his nose.

You're too `little` to help me.

- The children can find other words in the story which could be treated in this way, such as *big, gnawed* and *eat*.

- They can experiment with writing these words, and use them in a rewrite of the story.

- Investigate other books which make special use of type; for example, *Chicken Little* and *The Fox and the Little Red Hen*.

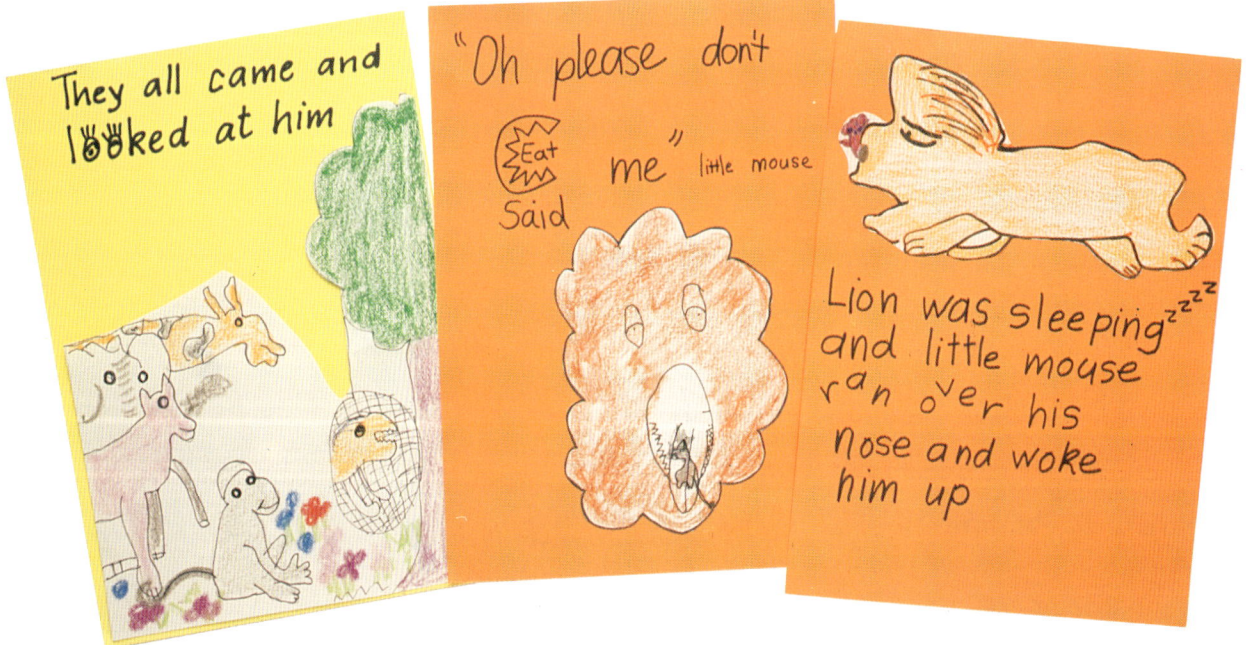

Making a rebus title

Visual thinking

- Show the children some traditional story titles in pictures rather than words, such as *The* 🐷🐷🐷 or *Jack and the* 🌱.

- The children can work in pairs to design a rebus title for *The Lion and the Mouse*. Share and display.

- As a follow-up, the children can create a rebus story.

Making a collage wall story

Art and language

- Collect a variety of textured materials, such as fabrics, string, embossed wallpaper, bark and leaves.

- Brainstorm the story's main events; list these.

- The children can select an event to show in collage form.

- Have the children put the collages in sequence and write captions for them.

- Display the collages as a wall story. Have the children describe each other's work using terms that relate to texture, shape and size.

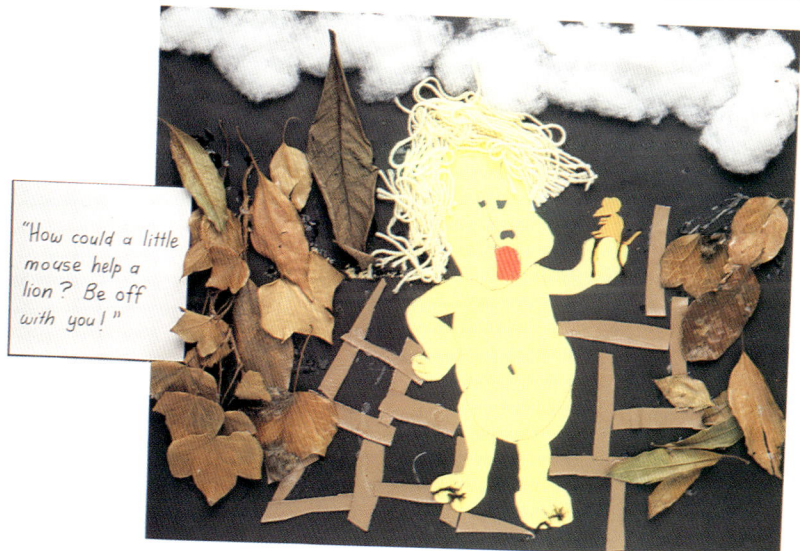

"Please help me!" begged the lion. But the other animals just stood there.

"How could a little mouse help a lion? Be off with you!"

Making mouse T-shirts

Exploring signs and slogans

- Have the children design a T-shirt that might be awarded to Mouse for rescuing Lion.

- Display their T-shirt designs, and invite other classes to the exhibition.

- As a follow-up, the children can investigate other signs, slogans and labels on clothing; for example, sports clothing and laundry and manufacturers' labels.

Big and small

Mathematics (measurement and comparison)

- Give each child a copy of Blackline Master 7; have them colour the lion and the mouse and cut them out.

- Have the children find things that are wider/narrower than the mouse, and longer/shorter than the lion.

- They can then record and discuss their findings.

A circle story

Exploring story structure

- Brainstorm and list the main events in the story.

- Have the children select an event, then work in groups to illustrate and describe it.

- They can then arrange the events into a circle story.

- As a follow-up, take the children on an excursion; afterwards, discuss what you saw and have the children make a circle story of their journey.

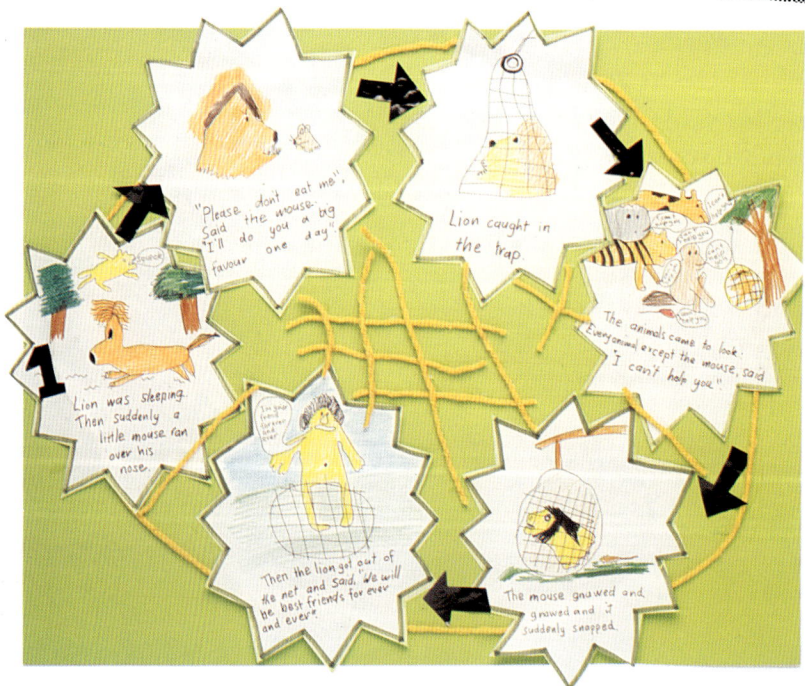

Making a helping book

Language and social studies

- Brainstorm a class list of people who help us, such as doctors, teachers and bus drivers.

- The children can select someone from the list and record how and where that person helps them.

- The children's work can be put together to form a big book, entitled *Our Helping Book.*

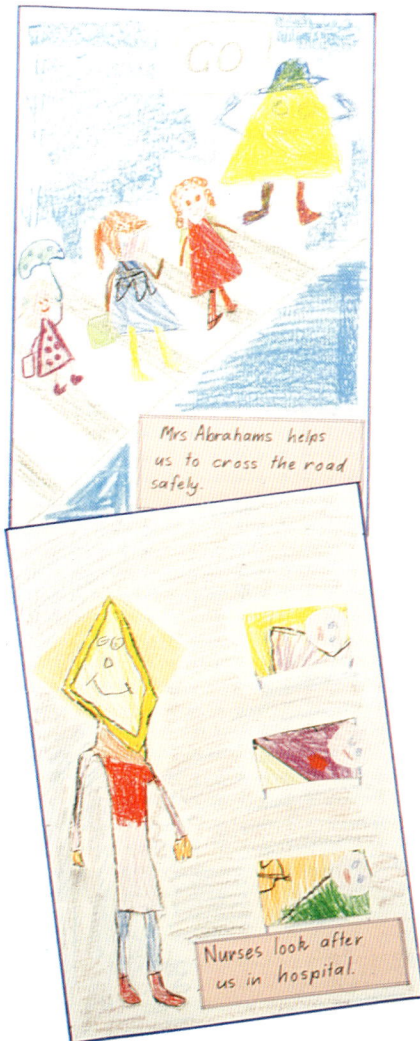

Mrs Abrahams helps us to cross the road safely.

Nurses look after us in hospital.

Help Lion escape

Problem solving

- Discuss how Mouse helped Lion to escape.

- List the other animals in the story and their attributes. *Could these animals have helped Lion?*

- The children can select an animal, then illustrate and describe how that animal might have helped Lion.

- Share and compare the solutions.

The giraffe could have put it's long neck under the net and it would roll down the giraffe's neck and it would snap when it hit the ground

The tiger could have climbed up the tree and put all his weight on the branch and snapped it.

All the animals could have helped by pulling and pulling until the lion said, "I will scratch it and it will snap."

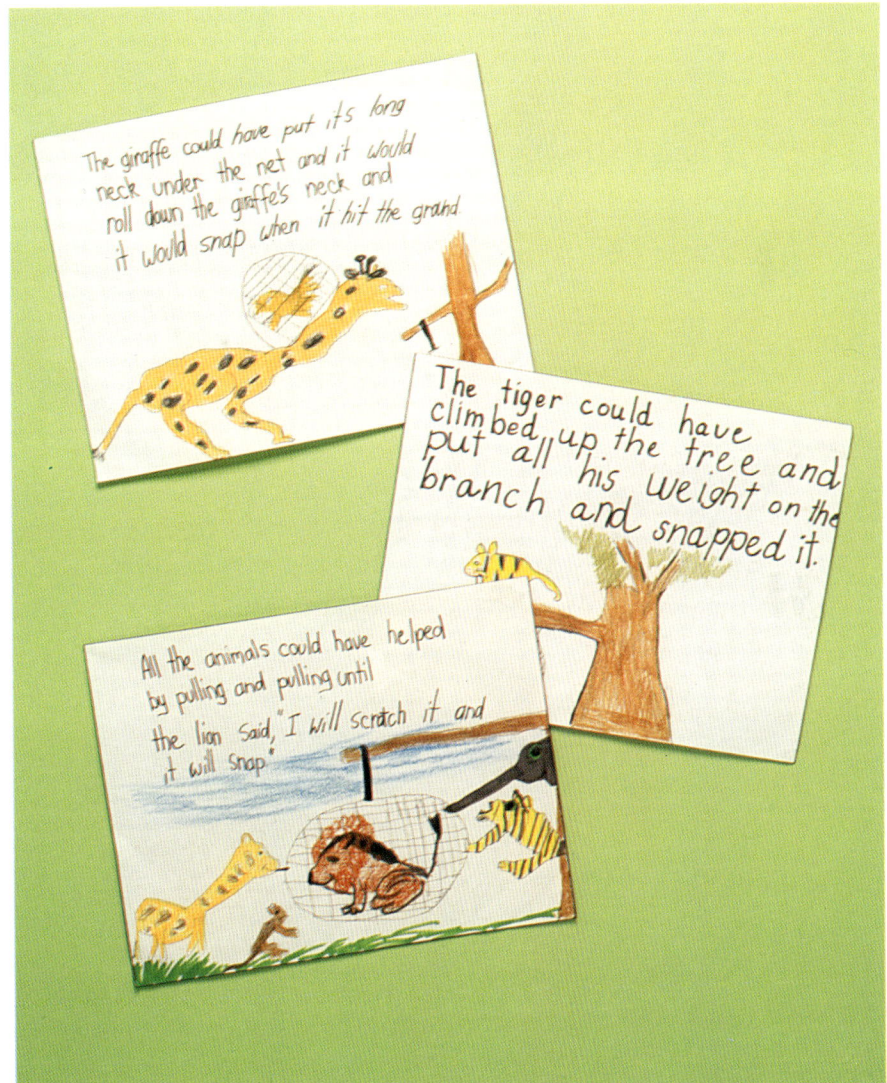

Other suggestions

- Classify the animals in as many ways as possible.
- Consider how other animals in traditional stories were helped.
- Find a poem about a lion or a mouse.

33

Chicken Little

Chicken Little's appeal lies in its cast of endearingly foolish characters, and in its use of a cumulative and repetitive story structure. Children will also enjoy exploring mathematical and scientific concepts arising from the story, and participating in related art and language activities.

The further adventures of Chicken Little

Language (creative writing)

- *What happened to Chicken Little after she returned safely to the farm?* Discuss some possibilities.

- The children can write and illustrate the further adventures of Chicken Little.

- Share and display the children's stories, or compile them into a book.

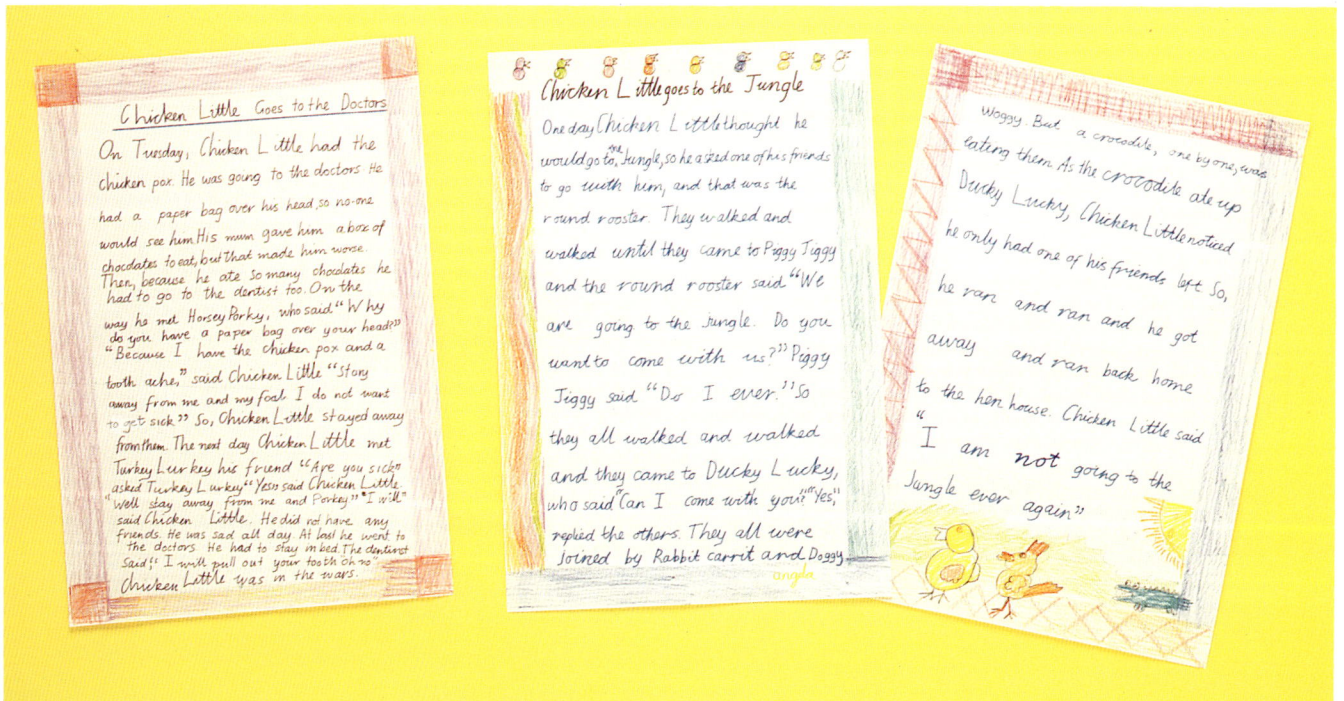

Animal facts

Science

- Review the types of birds in *Chicken Little* and make a list of them.
- Brainstorm lists of each bird's features.
- Have the children select birds and work in groups to find out more about them; they can then record in chart form the information they find.
- As a follow-up, the children can create similar charts for other animals, adding more information over time.

Which bird is that?

Writing factual descriptions

- After the *Animal Facts* activity, have the children write their own descriptions of birds. They can base these on the charts and conduct extra research if required.
- The children can illustrate and share their writing.

Same and different

Science and mathematics (graphing)

- Compare and discuss the birds on the *Animal Facts* charts. *How are they similar? How are they different?*
- The children can research differences between birds, such as how much they eat, how much they weigh and how many eggs they lay. This information can be presented in graph form.

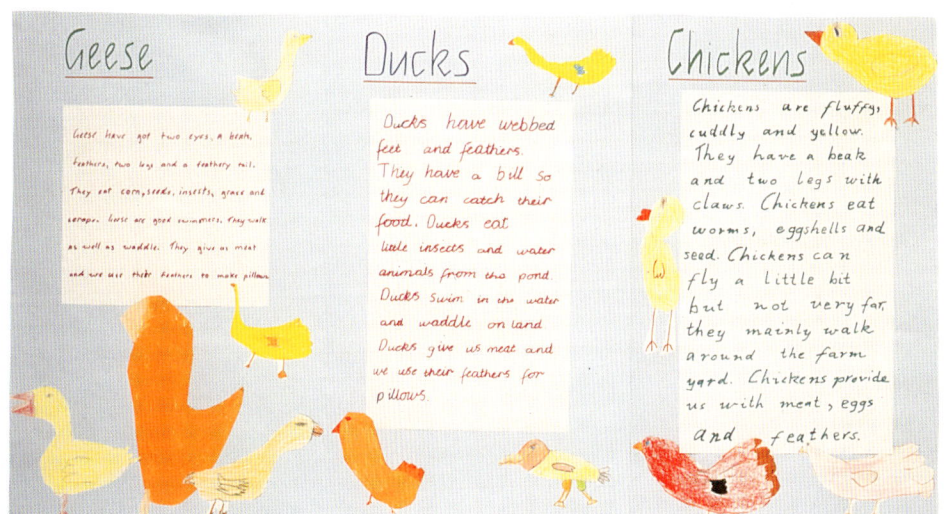

Illustrating the story

Art

- Collect a variety of collage materials, such as wrapping paper, magazines, bark and leaves.

- Discuss with the children which scene they would like to illustrate.

- Tape several large sheets of paper together, sketch the scene onto them and have the children paint the backdrop.

- The children can then decide which collage materials suit each character, and work on a section of the mural over several days.

- Note: In the above collage, the turkey's tail was made from hand-shapes cut from paper; the duck was made from crepe paper rolled into balls; and the goose was made by pasting on cotton wool balls.

Find the way

Mathematics (visual thinking)

- Give each child a copy of Blackline Master 8.

- The children need to help Chicken Little find a path to the King's castle via her friends', while avoiding Foxy Loxy. There is more than one solution.

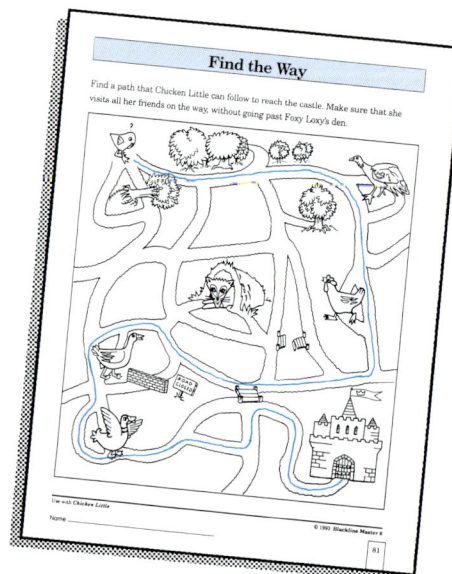

Making pompom chickens

Art and language (following instructions)

- Prepare a chart telling the children how to make pompom chickens (as shown). Have the children follow the steps.

- Use the finished pompom chickens in a play version of the story, or display them as mobiles.

HOW TO MAKE
POMPOM CHICKENS

What you will need:
- 2 cardboard circles with holes
- Wool — lots of it
- Scissors
- Glue
- Marking pens
- Extra cardboard for head and feet

What to do:

1 Take the 2 circles.

2 Wind wool evenly around them.

3 Cover the circles completely.

4 Hold the card firmly and cut around the edges.

5 Ease the 2 pieces of cardboard apart and tie a piece of wool inside.

6 Glue on cardboard head and feet.

Loud and soft

Exploring onomatopoeia

- Discuss some words which sound like their meanings, such as CHOMP!

- The children can compile lists of loud words and soft words. These can be displayed in a chart and used as a wordbank for the children's own writing.

Loud and soft words

LOUD	soft
BANG	creep
CRASH	whisper
EXPLODE	tippy toe
YELL	secrets
BASH	sleep

The Three Billy Goats Gruff

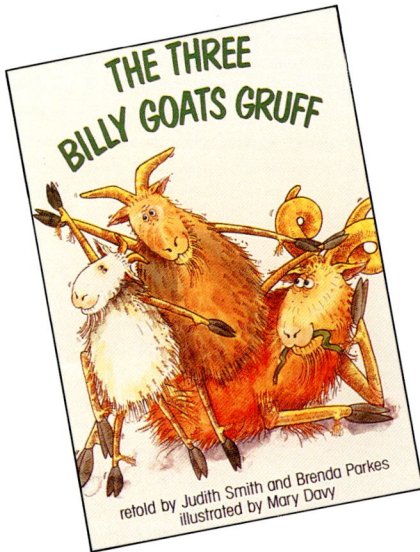

THE THREE
BILLY GOATS GRUFF

retold by Judith Smith and Brenda Parkes
illustrated by Mary Davy

The Three Billy Goats Gruff is popular with children of all ages. Its lively text, which features repetitive language and onomatopoeia, is a springboard to a wide range of challenging activities, incorporating art, mathematics, social studies, drama and music.

Building a bridge

Art and mathematics

- Collect pictures of bridges to share. Discuss where and why bridges are used.

- Collect boxes and other materials that the children can use to build model bridges of their own design.

- The children can work in groups to build their bridges, then share their models and tell about their design. For example, bridges could be described in terms of shapes, patterns or the number of pieces used in their construction.

- As a follow-up, have the children write "how-to" instructions for their bridges.

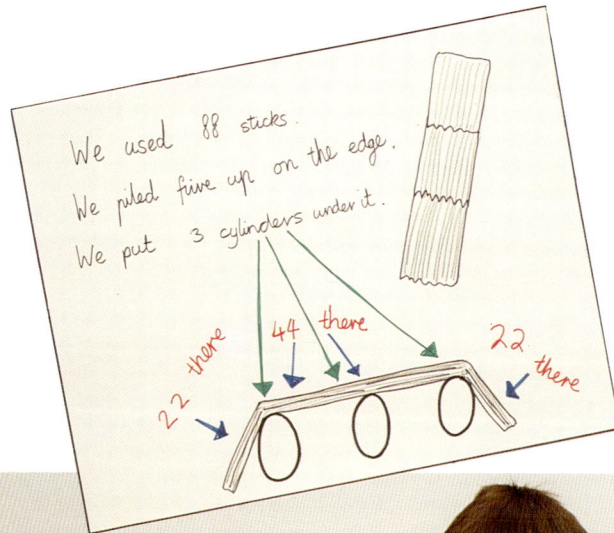

We used 88 sticks.
We piled five up on the edge.
We put 3 cylinders under it.

22 there   44 there   22 there

Keep off !

Language and social studies

- Discuss signs that the children see at school and in the local environment. *What do they look like? What do they tell us?*

- Explore signs that use symbols not words. *What advantages do these have?*

- The children can design signs warning the goats to keep off the troll's bridge.

- Later, the class can vote for their favourite signs, then tally and graph the results.

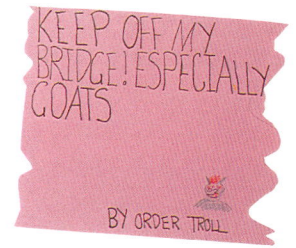

Troll tales

Imaginative writing

- Brainstorm ideas for new stories that include trolls. Encourage the children to use their imaginations freely in inventing new storylines and settings — even outer space.

- Select an idea to develop as a class story. Write and edit the text together and then have the children work in groups to plan and carry out the illustrations.

- The story can be displayed in sequence as a wall story, or the pages can be bound together to form a book.

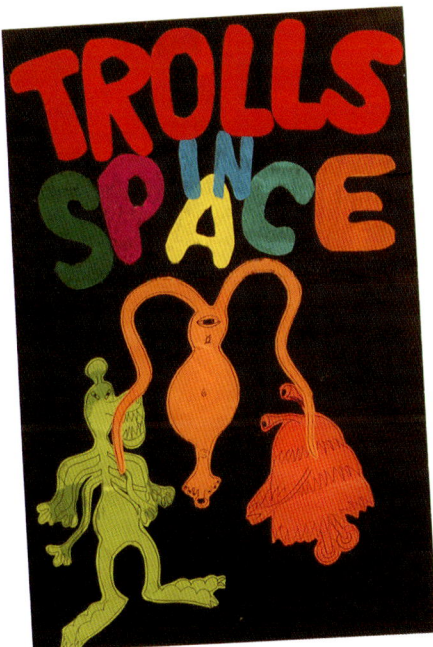

Finding a way

Problem solving

- *Could the goats and the troll have come to an agreement about using the bridge? Could the goats have crossed elsewhere? Discuss these and similar questions as a class.*

- Discuss any current real-world disputes that the children may be aware of.

Share ideas about how these might be resolved.

- The children can select an issue and work in groups to respond to it. This could involve writing to a local newspaper or radio station, designing posters or raising funds.

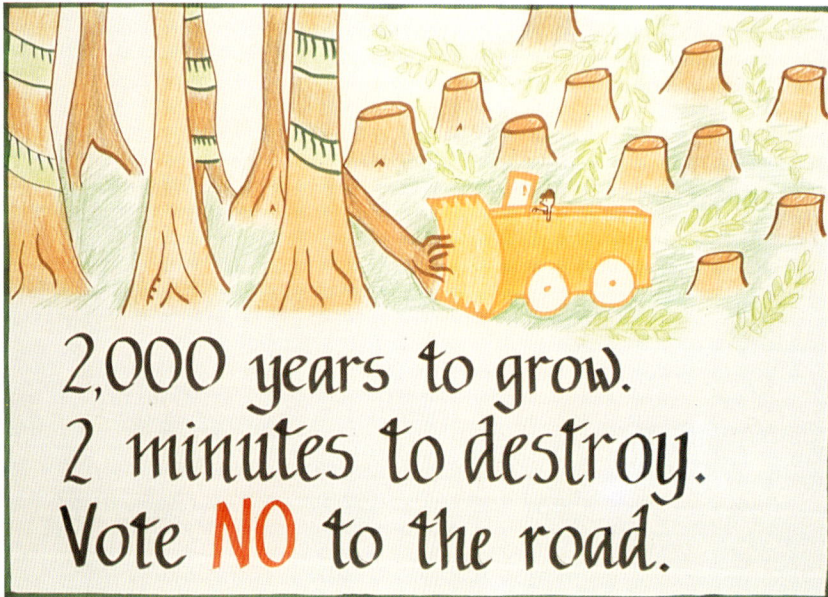

2,000 years to grow.
2 minutes to destroy.
Vote NO to the road.

Just the facts

Language (investigating newspaper reporting)

- Give each child a copy of Blackline Master 9. Read the examples aloud. *What do you think happened next?*

- The children can select a headline and an opening sentence (or invent their own), then write the rest of the story.

- As a follow-up, discuss newspaper language.

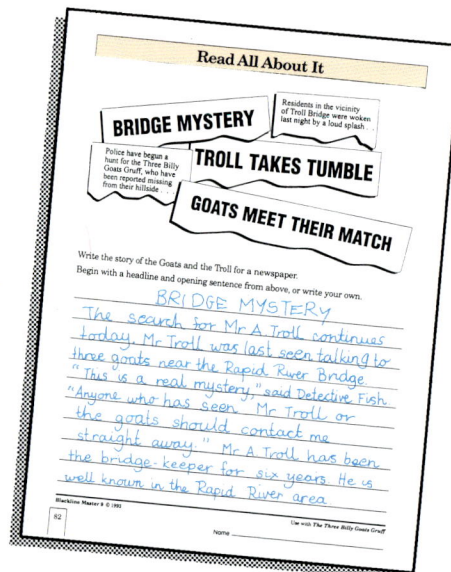

I'm mean when ...

Comparative stories and points of view

- Collect traditional tales that feature mean or bad-tempered characters; for example, *Jack and the Beanstalk* and *The Three Little Pigs.*

- Discuss the characters. *Do they have anything in common? Do they have reasons for being bad-tempered?*

- The children could use role play to tell about the character from their points of view.

- Then ask the children, *What makes you grumpy?* Discuss their responses and then have them choose a situation to write about and illustrate.

I'm grumpy when no-one plays with me.

Making a diorama

Art and drama

- This diorama uses a small cardboard box as a stage for retelling the story. Plastic bags stuffed with crumpled newspaper can form the hills; suitably-coloured paper and fabric scraps can form the earth, grass and river; and the backdrop can be painted or collaged.

- To make marionettes, cut out cardboard for the characters' bodies and heads; these can be covered with fabric scraps or "fur". Limbs can be made from pipe cleaners, stockings or craft sticks. Use wool for the strings, and attach a handle so that the puppets can be moved easily.

I've got rhythm

Music

- Discuss how sound effects could be added to the story. Which noises would suit the different characters?

- The children can make their own instruments; for example, "guitars" can be made by stretching rubber bands over holes in plastic containers; "xylophones" can be made by filling bottles to different levels and tapping them with spoons; other percussion instruments can be made from woodblocks or kitchen utensils.

Other suggestions

- Have the children brainstorm other ways for the goats to cross the river, such as using flying foxes and rafts.
- Design a Three Billy Goats Gruff board game.
- Write the troll's diary.

The Fisherman and His Wife

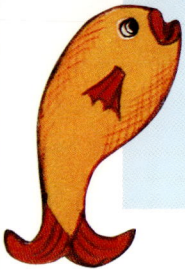

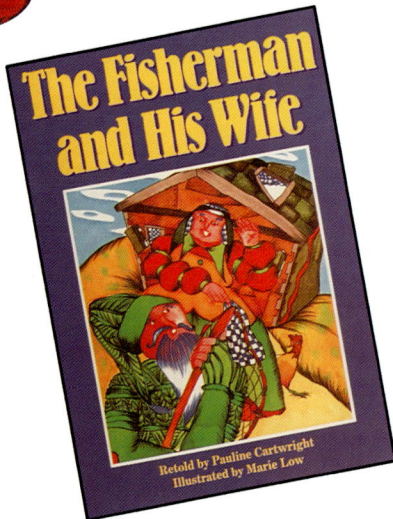

The Fisherman and His Wife is a powerful story revolving around greed and its outcomes. The repetitive nature of the story, with the hapless fisherman returning again and again to the sea to ask the same question, helps the reader to predict the conclusion. The story's setting and plot provide the opportunity for a diverse range of classroom activities.

Front page news

Exploring the language and form of newspapers

- Collect local newspapers and share some of the news items.
- Discuss the format of newspapers; for example, how columns are used, and how headlines, stories and pictures are set out.
- Brainstorm ideas for a newspaper story about the fisherman. Write the story as a class.
- Make up a name for a class newspaper, and create suitable advertisements and illustrations.

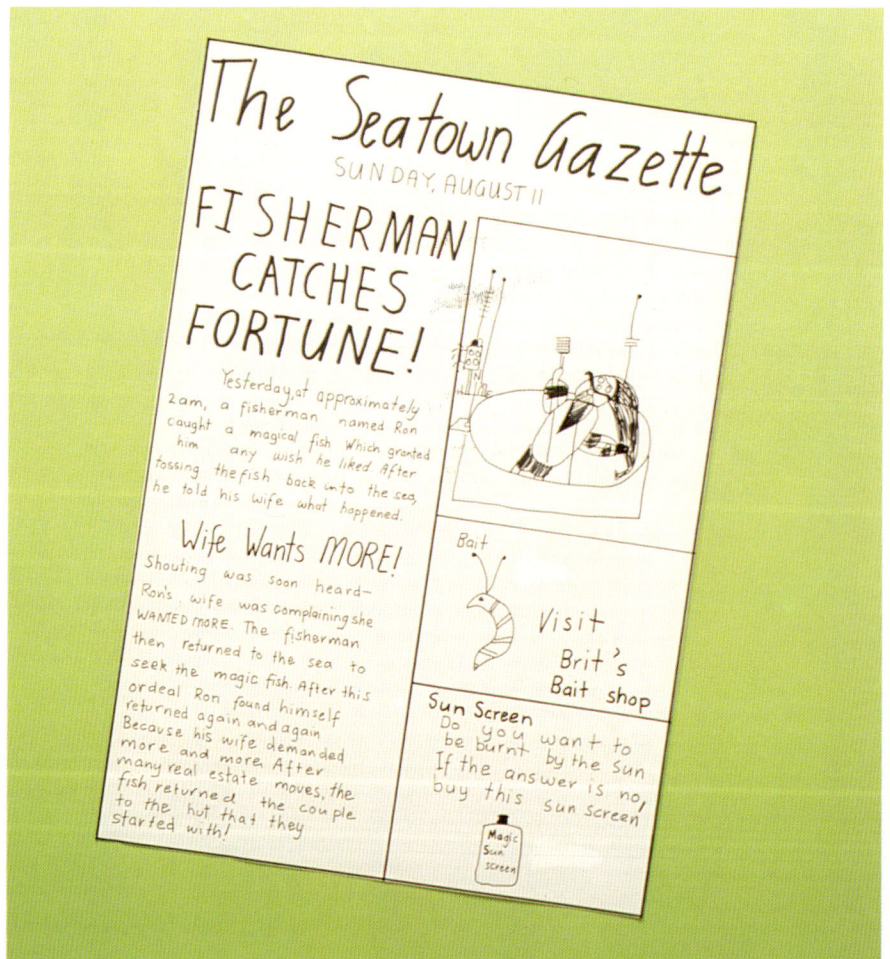

Keeping a diary

Exploring character through personal writing

- Explore how diaries are structured, and their use of first person ("I"). Model some examples.

- Discuss the fisherman. *What might he have written in his diary?*

- The children can write the fisherman's diary, based on the story's events.

- As a follow-up, the children can use diary writing to record class and personal events.

Monday

My wife nagged for a magic wish.
I didn't want to go but I went.
So I called,
"Oh fantastic fish, Oh fantastic fish, Please grant my wife a magic wish."
My wife got a nice house.

Tuesday

My wife longed for an Enchanted wis[h]
So I went. I d[idn't] want to go but [in the] end I went. So I [called,]
"Oh fantastic fish, Oh fantastic fish My wife nags a magic wish."
My wife got wh[at] she wanted.

Wednesday

My wife wanted another wish. So I went and called all over again. My wife got her wish.

Floating and sinking

Science (investigating properties)

- Fill a large container with water.

- Collect a range of items which sink or float; for example, corks, toy boats, teaspoons and rocks.

- The children can predict if the items will float or sink.

- After checking their predictions, they can sort the items into groups and discuss the results.

Making a fisherman

Art and language

- The children can draw a body outline for the fisherman on thin card, and then "clothe" him by pasting on fabric scraps.

- Brainstorm words that describe the fisherman's thoughts and feelings; write these on labels and attach them to the collage figure.

poor

honest

humble

scared

afraid

hard worker

unwilling

Changing places

Exploring character

- Collect large plastic bottles, fabric scraps, stockings and foam or crumpled newspapers.

- Discuss the appearance of the fisherman's wife and how it changes with her status. *What kinds of fabrics could be used to show these changes?*

- The children can work in groups to make suitably dressed models of the fisherman's wife for each of her stages:
  — make the head by stuffing foam or crumpled newspaper into a stocking and tying securely;
  — tape the head to the neck of the bottle and draw on features;
  — make dresses and cloaks from fabric pieces.

- The children can write captions and dialogue for the models, or use them for retelling the story.

Safe and sure

Exploring safety issues

- Discuss beaches and various types of beach activities.

- Brainstorm a list of items needed for safety on the beach; these might relate to sun protection or water safety.

- Make up a beach safety poster and have the children draw and label appropriate safety features, such as sunscreen and hats. Share and display.

- To follow up, the children can bring labels from home and make a collage on safety products.

Dear Magic Fish

Language (letter writing, point of view)

- Discuss the fisherman's feelings. *Does he want to ask the Magic Fish for more wishes? Is he afraid to go back to the sea? How does he feel at the end of the story?*

- The children can write letters to the Magic Fish on the fisherman's behalf, giving his point of view.

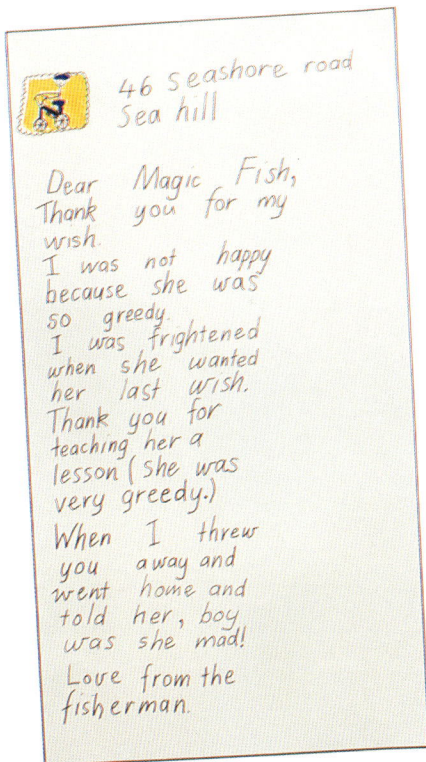

> 46 seashore road
> Sea hill
>
> Dear Magic Fish,
> Thank you for my wish.
> I was not happy because she was so greedy.
> I was frightened when she wanted her last wish.
> Thank you for teaching her a lesson (she was very greedy.)
> When I threw you away and went home and told her, boy was she mad!
> Love from the fisherman.

What other characters wanted

Exploring links between stories

- Discuss the fisherman's wife. *What did she want?*

- The children can compare the fisherman's wife with characters in other stories. *Did other characters want anything as badly as she did?* For example, Cinderella wanted to go to the ball; the Billy Goats Gruff wanted to eat grass.

- Share and compare stories to find other common themes; these can be used as the basis for the children's own stories.

Other suggestions

- The children can make fish mobiles.
- Compile a class book of fish facts.
- Read and compare other versions of this story.
- Write a diary from the fisherman's wife's point of view.
- Write about people who work by the sea, such as light-house keepers, sailors and coastguards.
- Make a display about ways of spending leisure time by the sea.

45

Rumpelstiltskin

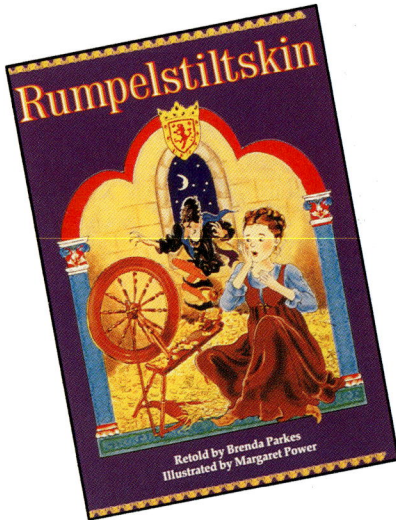

The story of Rumpelstiltskin, with the terrible predicament of the girl faced with the impossible task of spinning straw into gold, never fails to capture the imagination of young readers. Its strong plot and clearly defined characters draw readers into the story and lead naturally into a wide range of classroom activities.

A wall story

Art and language

- Collect fabric offcuts of varying shape, colour and texture.
- Brainstorm the story's main events; list these.
- Have the children work in groups; they can select an event and illustrate it by pasting fabric offcuts on a painted background.
- Sequence the events and display them as a wall story with captions and/or labels.

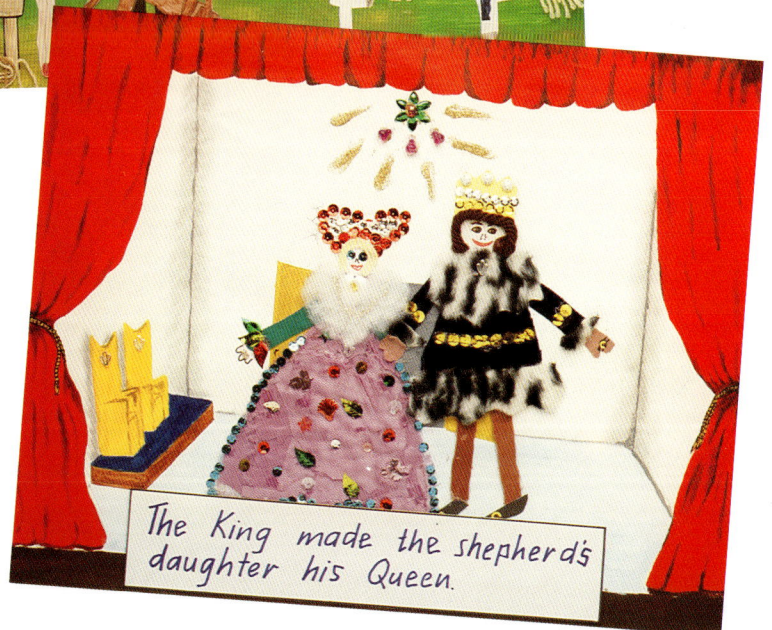

"My daughter can spin straw into gold," boasted the shepherd.

The King made the shepherd's daughter his Queen.

Help me

Exploring characters' emotions

- As a class, consider the plight of the shepherd's daughter. *How would you feel in her situation? Angry? Sad? Confused?* Discuss other characters in a similar way.

- The children can select and illustrate a scene from the story, adding speech bubbles to show the characters' feelings.

- Alternatively, the children can write "emotion" labels for their drawings of the characters.

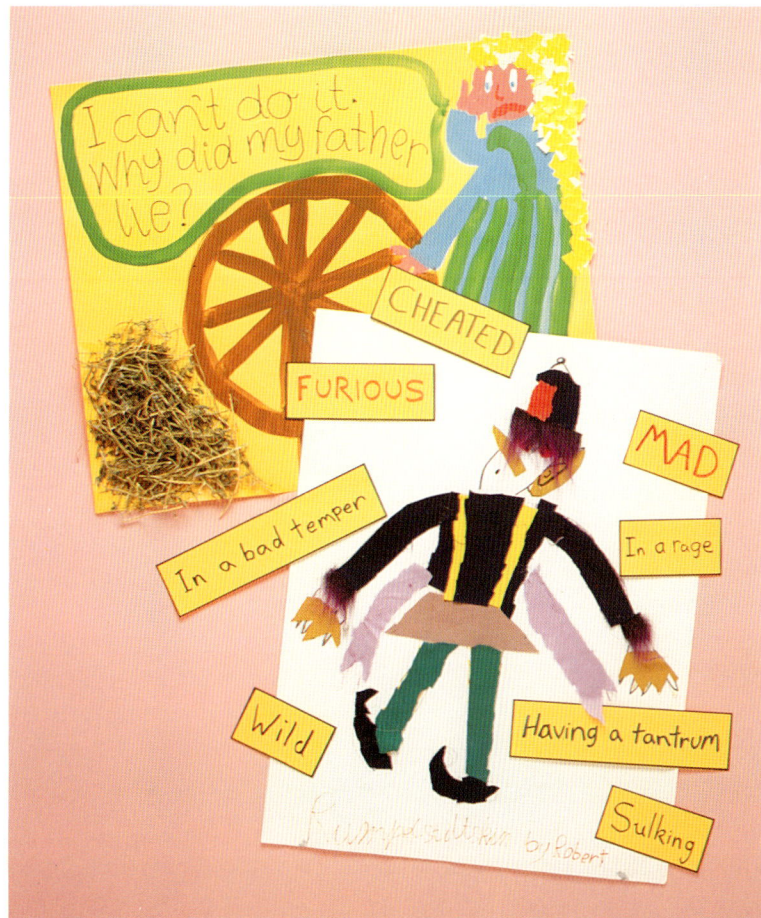

I was happy when . . .

Exploring our emotions

- Discuss different emotions and when the children feel them.

- Encourage the children to describe a time when they felt a strong emotion, such as happiness, embarrassment or sadness.

- Have the children write about and illustrate one emotion.

- Share and display the stories.

Creatures that spin

Science: research

- Make a list of creatures that spin (spiders, silkworms).
- Investigate how they spin and for what purposes (travel, food, to make homes).
- Collect discarded webs, nests, cocoons and other spun homes and bring them to the classroom for display.
- The children can research facts about creatures that spin; these can be illustrated and compiled into a book.

Ways with weaving

Art

- Collect a variety of yarns and fabrics; examine how they are made, and discuss spinning and weaving.
- The children can experiment with different types of weaving: for example, *branch weaving,* which involves weaving fabric strips around a forked branch; *net weaving,* which uses onion or orange bags; and *paper plate weaving,* where yarn is threaded through holes punched in a paper plate.
- Incorporate weaving into follow-up activities; for example, using woven place mats as table decorations for a Royal Banquet.

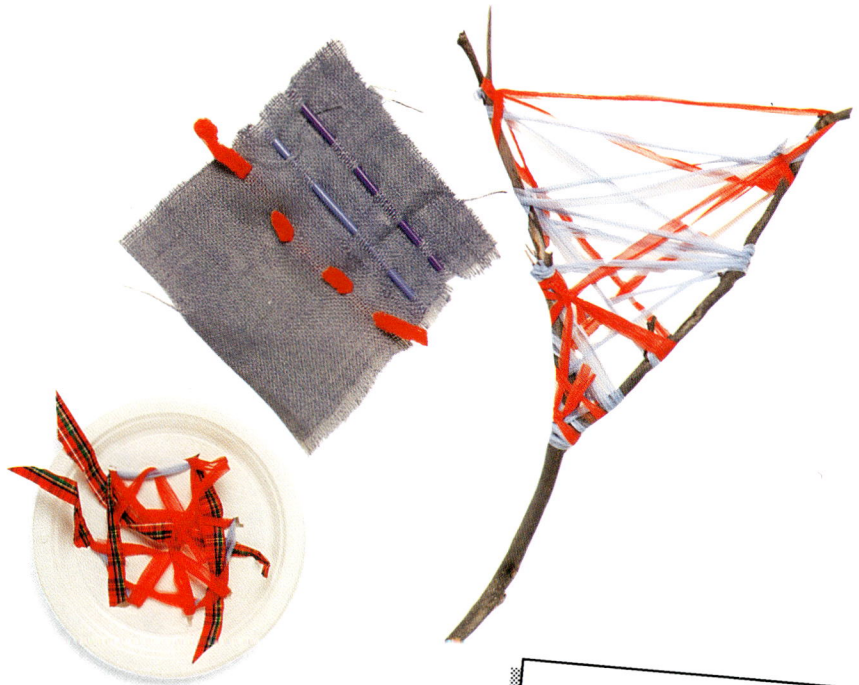

Find the words

Expanding vocabulary

- Give each child a copy of Blackline Master 10. There are 20 words to find, all made from Rumpelstiltskin's name.
- Later, the children might like to create wonderword puzzles based on other stories.

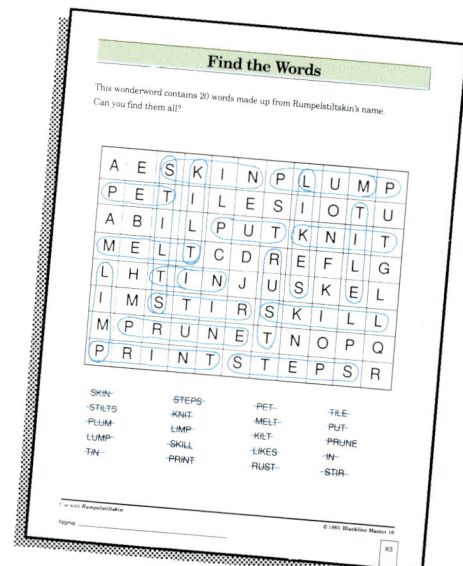

Nonsense names

Language and art

- *What might the name Rumpelstiltskin mean?* Brainstorm and discuss some possibilities.

- Have the children form new words by joining words or sounds not normally linked — such as Rumpelstiltskin.

- Have the children draw pictures and label them with their "new" words.

- They can invent meanings for their words; compile these into a fun dictionary.

Making a map

Visual thinking

- Review the book; ask the children questions about where the story is set and where the characters live.

- Have the children draw and label maps of the story's setting. These could include the King's castle, the forest where Rumpelstiltskin lives and the shepherd's house.

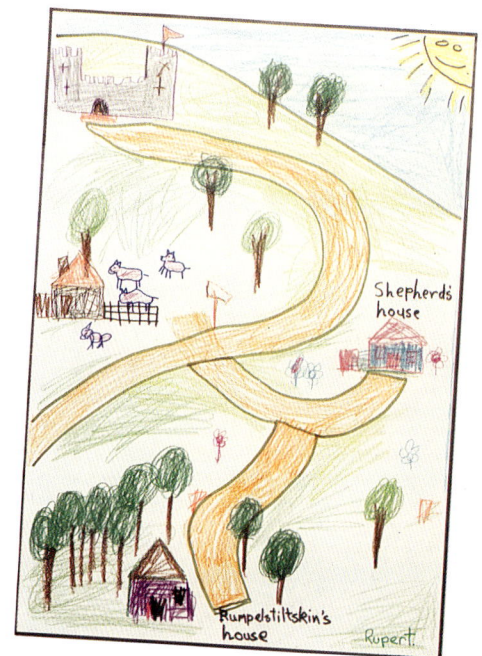

- Share and display.

Other suggestions

- Find different versions of the story and compare them.
- The children can put on a performance of Rumpelstiltskin.

Jack and the Beanstalk

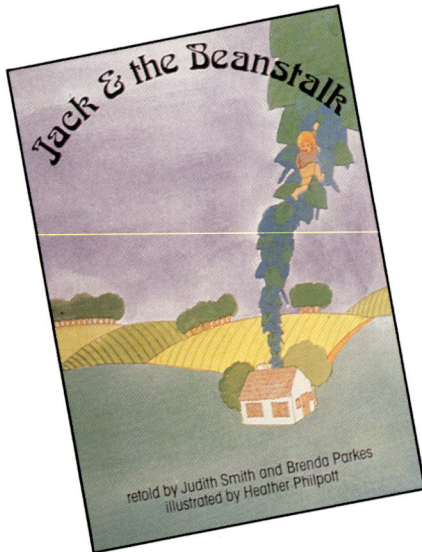

Jack and the Beanstalk brings together many of the features that draw children into the world of traditional tales. Along with its memorable chant of *Fe fi fo fum*, it offers themes of magic, trickery and rags to riches, all within a strong episodic story structure. The possibilities for reader response are endless.

Making and describing a giant

Art, language and mathematics (measurement)

- Collect scrap materials such as vinyl, carpet scraps, old buttons, yarn and foil.

- Help the children to draw a large outline for a giant —you could lie down on paper to provide a model!

- Have the children arrange and then paste various scrap materials to fill the outline.

- Discuss and write several words to describe the giant and attach these to the figure. The children can add more labels over time.

- Discuss and explore other ways of describing the giant; for example, using measurement ideas.

Dialogues and mini-scripts

Writing and performance

- Pairs of children can select episodes related to the story and write the conversations that might have occurred.

- The children can explore different ways of doing this, such as a story with direct speech or a play script.

- Encourage the children to act out their scripts and stories; role-plays and performances will bring their work to life.

- As a follow-up, combine the children's scripts and put on a class performance of *Jack and the Beanstalk*.

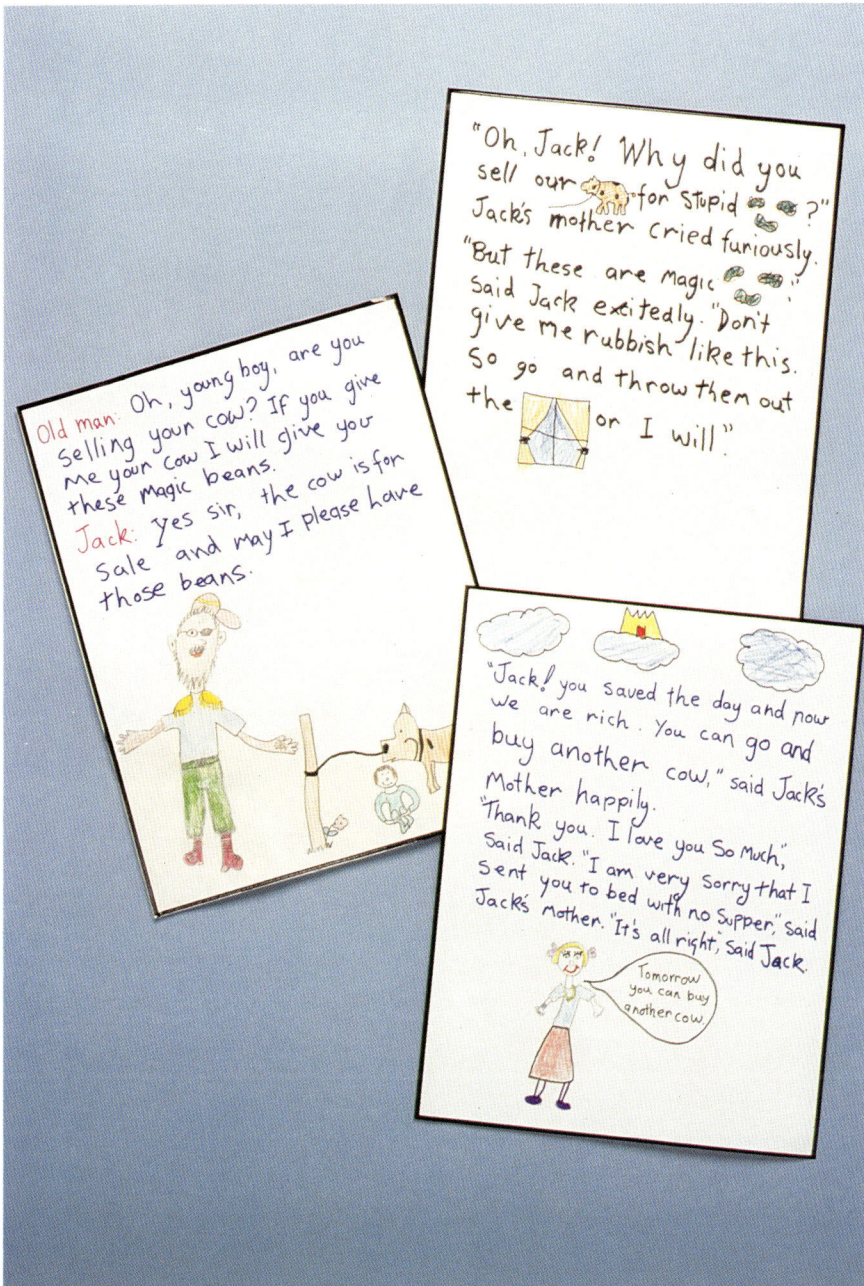

Favourite episodes

Art and language

- Provide a variety of collage materials, paints and crayons.

- The children can select their favourite parts of the story and illustrate these.

- Encourage them to include labels, captions and thought bubbles in their creations.

- Share and discuss the children's work; encourage them to tell why they liked some parts of the story more than others.

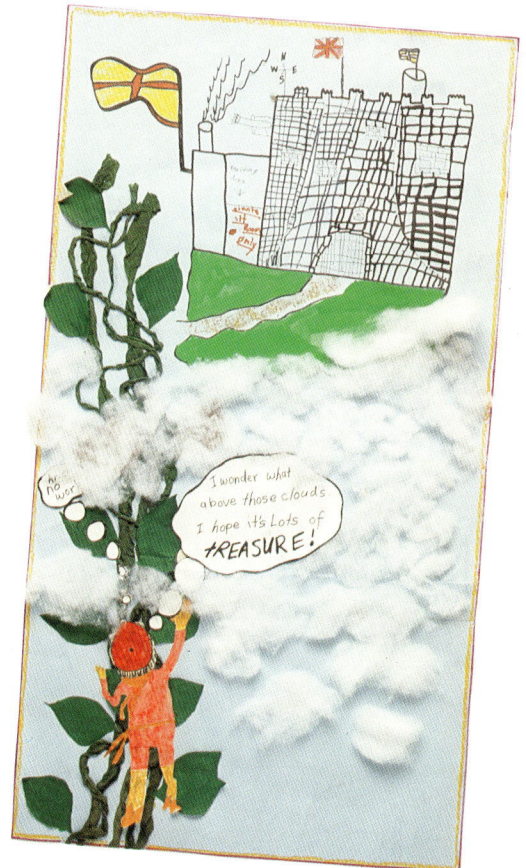

Growing and graphing beans

Mathematics (measurement and graphing)

- Soak dried beans overnight.
- The children can line a glass jar with cotton wool; the beans are then put between the cotton wool and the glass.
- Moisten the cotton wool and place the jar in the light. Keep the cotton wool damp.
- The class can then record and graph the beans' growth.
- Alternatively, collect a variety of vegetables that have seeds. Ask the children to predict what the seeds will be like: many or few, large or small. Open the vegetables, and display and count the seeds. The children can record the information in a graph.

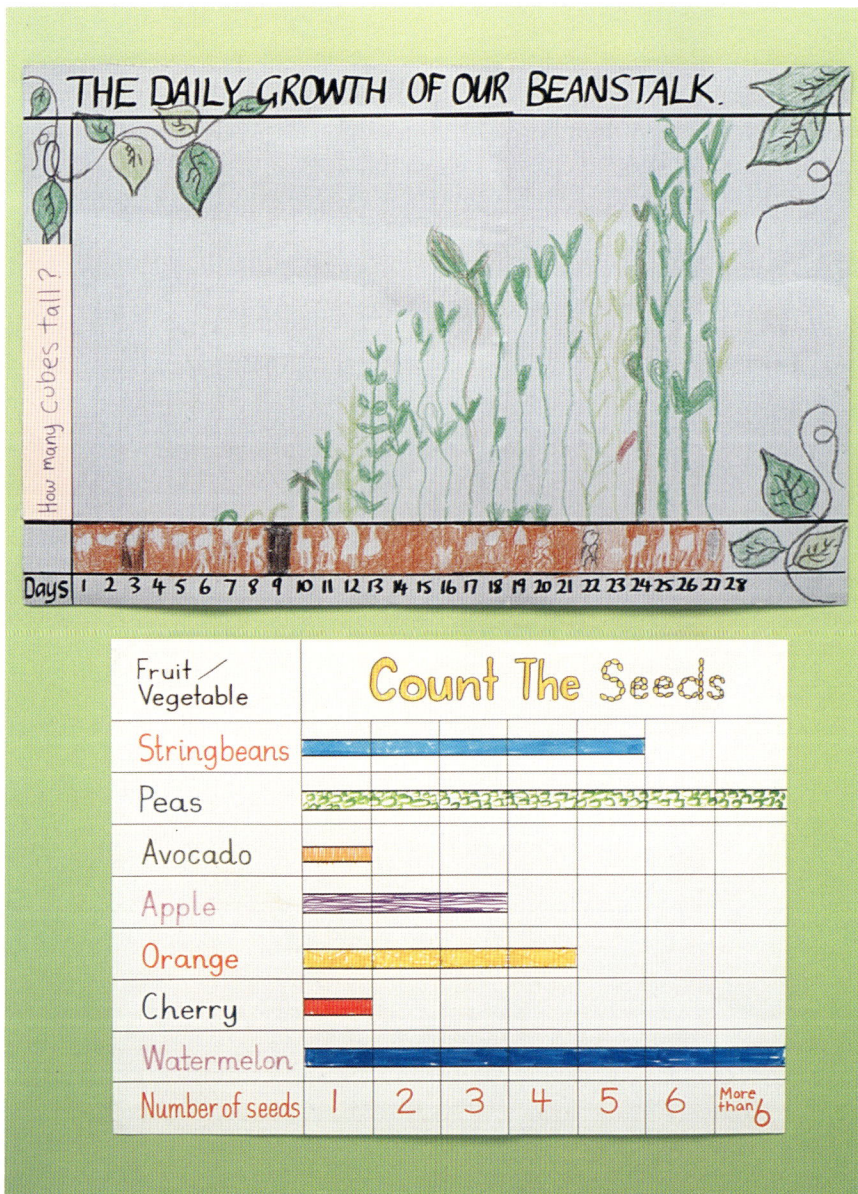

THE DAILY GROWTH OF OUR BEANSTALK.

How many cubes tall?

Days | 1 2 3 4 5 6 7 8 9 10 11 12 13 14 15 16 17 18 19 20 21 22 23 24 25 26 27 28

Fruit / Vegetable	Count The Seeds					
Stringbeans						
Peas						
Avocado						
Apple						
Orange						
Cherry						
Watermelon						
Number of seeds	1	2	3	4	5	6 More than 6

Problem solving

Exploring different solutions

- Display a page from the book and ask the children to tell what is happening.
- Pose some open-ended questions and encourage possible solutions. For example, look at pages 16-17:

Ask the class questions such as, *Is there anywhere Jack could hide the gold? What would the Giant have said if he woke up? What if Jack had dropped the bag of gold on the Giant's foot?*

Put similar questions on the bulletin board and let the children take turns writing suggestions.

What would the Giant have said if he woke up?

Ah, supper!
Fe fi fo fum!
Aaargh! A mouse!
Who's stealing my gold?

A song for Jack

Investigating other language forms

- Collect ballads and songs that tell stories; share these with the children.

- Encourage the children to write their own ballads based on favourite stories. Don't expect perfection in rhyme and rhythm — let the children be creative.

- Provide many opportunities for the children to present their work for the class, and to create musical accompaniments.

The Song of Jack and the Giant

Up up I climb, up the beanstalk as high as high
Then down I'll come with the treasure and gold and
when the giant comes down will chop it down.

I'm up at the castle so tall and high,
The giant is sleeping so I will not die,
But when he wakes up I'll shout and cry,
And then I'll run back home with the sugar and the pie.

Back I run, back I go, back to the castle where
the giant is close. The giant shouts out "Fe, Fi, Fo here
I go." I run back home and chop it down with the
saucer and pans.

These children are making musical instruments to accompany their songs.

Other suggestions

- Research and write about dairy cows; collect and display wrappers and labels from foods that are made from milk.

- The children can write alternative endings; for example, *What if Jack's mother had followed him?*

- Design tourist brochures for the Giant's kingdom in the clouds.

Puss-in-Boots

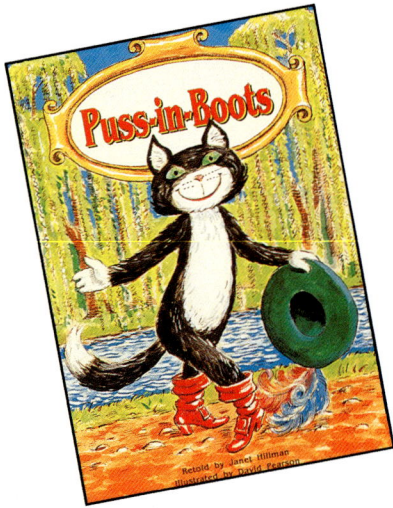

Puss-in-Boots introduces children to one of the most memorable "clever animals" of traditional tales. Familiar themes, such as adversity being turned into good fortune and a commoner marrying a princess, further add to the story's appeal. The plot involves many dramatic events which will help to inspire a range of activities.

Identifying key elements

Summarizing and sequencing

- Discuss the idea of making a story summary. *What needs to be included? What can be left out?* The children can write and illustrate their own summaries. Share and discuss.

- Discuss the time and sequence of events in the children's daily lives; for example, waking up, going to school and having lunch.

- The children can select and illustrate key events from their daily lives. They could draw clocks to show the time.

Picture this

Sequencing with pictures

- Discuss how the events in the story could be represented without using written language. Possibilities include drawing them in cartoon form or as a concertina book.
- The children can work in groups to plan and carry out their renditions of the story.
- Display the pictures and use them for retelling the story.

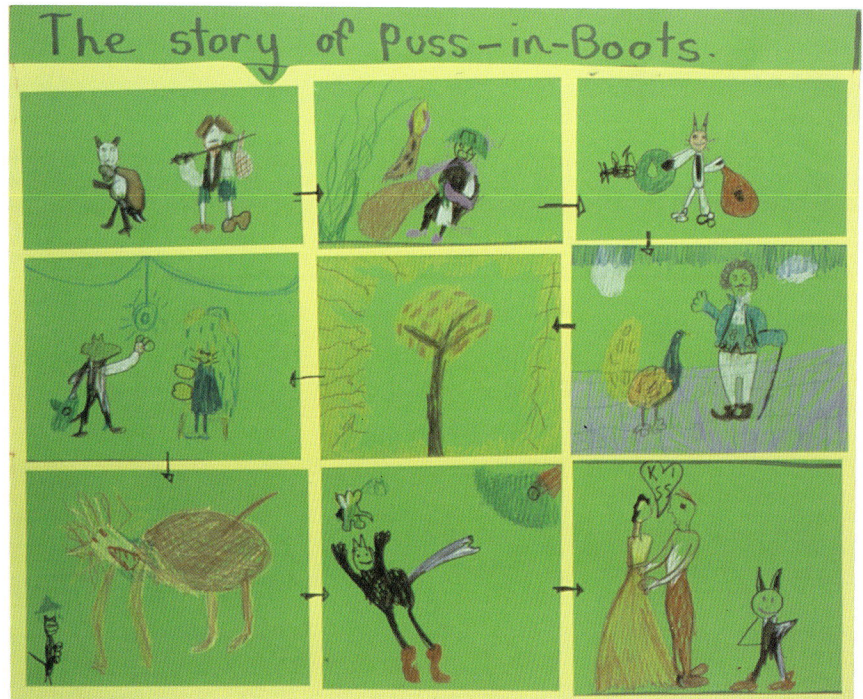

The story of Puss-in-Boots.

Rags to riches

Comparing stories

- Compare *Puss-in-Boots* with another traditional tale, such as *Cinderella*. Are there any similarities? For example, animals that talk, a youngest child, a poor person who becomes rich, marriage to a prince or princess, one thing that magically becomes another.
- The children can select one of these ideas to write about and illustrate.

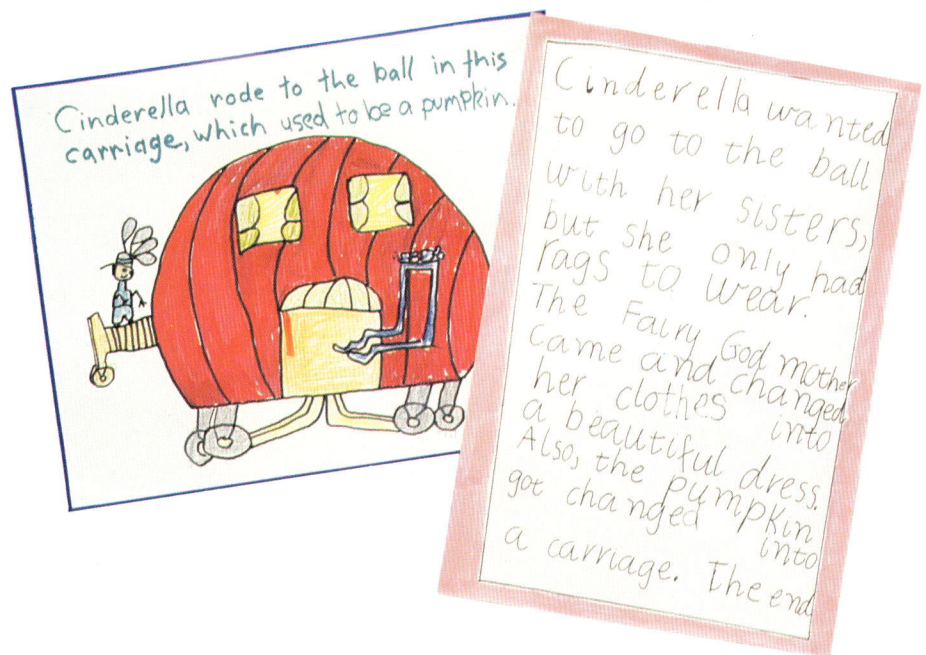

Cinderella rode to the ball in this carriage, which used to be a pumpkin.

Cinderella wanted to go to the ball with her sisters, but she only had rags to wear. The Fairy God mother came and changed her clothes into a beautiful dress. Also, the pumpkin got changed into a carriage. The end.

At Playtime I skip with my friends. We eat lunch. After School I play with my dog. I go to sleep.

Carriages and cars

Investigating transport

- Using the carriage that appears in *Puss-in-Boots* as a starting point, the children can investigate the design and use of carriages at different times in history.

- The children can go on to design their own carriages, or work in groups to investigate cars of different eras — past, present and future.

- The children can display their work around the classroom in chronological order.

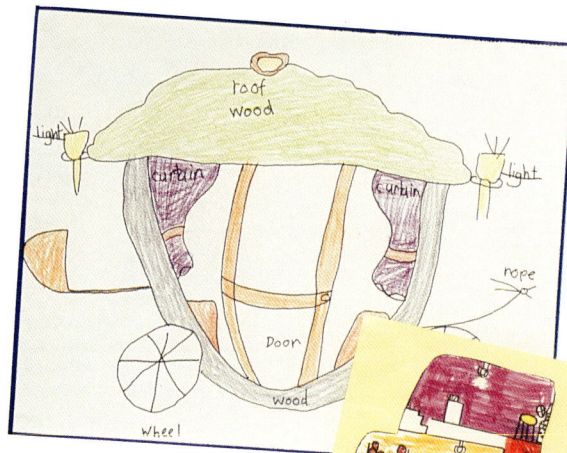

A peacock parade

Art

- Outline the peacocks on thin card. The children can then decorate them by pasting on shapes cut from fabric or paper, such as hands or ovals.

- Alternatively, cut holes in the card and paste cellophane behind them; they can then be taped to a window to form a display.

- As a follow-up, the children could compile a book of facts about peacocks. Add more facts over time.

The giant's castle

Art and mathematics (shapes, patterning)

- Share pictures of castles. *What features do they have in common?*

- Collect cardboard cylinders and boxes of various sizes that can be used for constructing castles.

- The children can work in groups to make and paint their castles.

- Discuss with the children how they made their castles and why they used the materials they did.

Castle mathematics

Writing about mathematics

- Select castles from *The Giant's Castle* activity, and explore different ways to describe them.

- Descriptions could focus on mathematical ideas; for example:
  — number; *This castle has 16 windows and 4 doors.*
  — comparison; *The second castle has more windows than the first.*
  — shapes; *My castle includes 4 cones, 4 cylinders and 1 cube.*

- The children can write mathematical statements; display these with the castles.

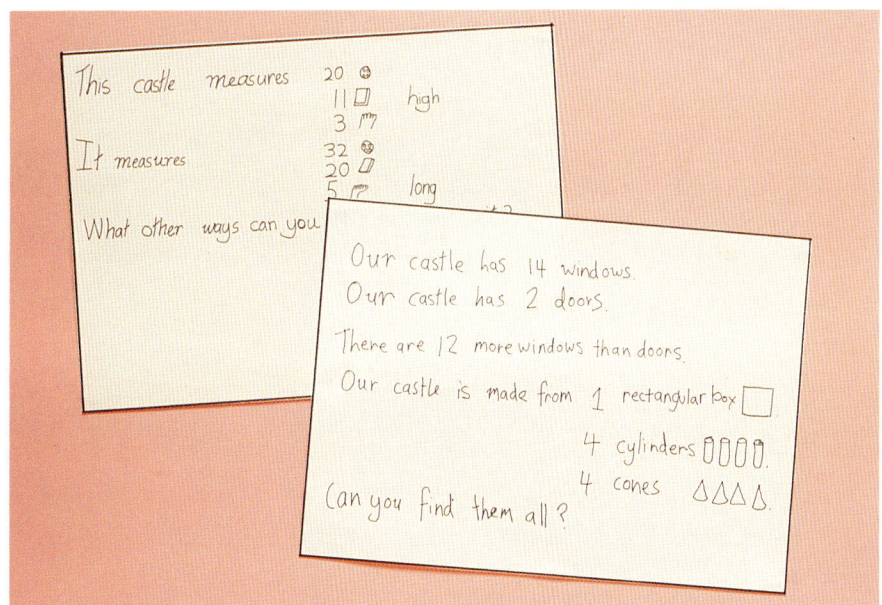

This castle measures 20 ⊕
                      11 ☐   high
                       3 ♩

It measures   32 ⊕
                      20 ▱
                       5 ▱   long

What other ways can you ...

Our castle has 14 windows.
Our castle has 2 doors.
There are 12 more windows than doors.
Our castle is made from 1 rectangular box ☐

                         4 cylinders ▯▯▯▯

Can you find them all?   4 cones △△△△

Other suggestions

- Write a report card for Puss-in-Boots.
- Write an alternative ending for the story.
- Design a poster for the film of *Puss-in-Boots*.
- Write a newspaper report on the Giant's death.
- Write "how-to" instructions for making a cardboard castle.

57

The Ugly Duckling

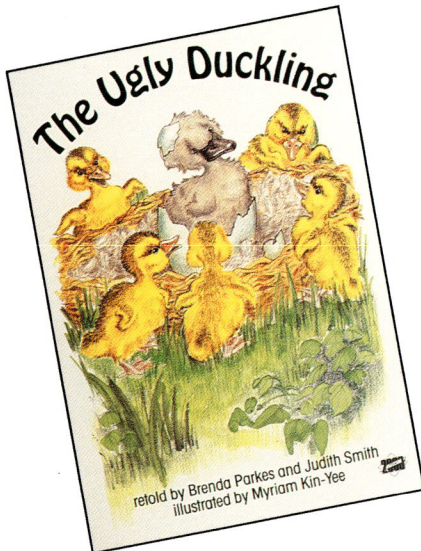

The Ugly Duckling
retold by Brenda Parkes and Judith Smith
illustrated by Myriam Kin-Yee

The Ugly Duckling is a well-known and popular story. Younger children, in particular, will strongly empathize with the Ugly Duckling's plight and his desire to be the same as the other ducks. The Ugly Duckling's characters, themes and strong episodic structure all provide great appeal and set the scene for a range of enjoyable activities.

All year round

Exploring the seasons

- Discuss the seasons of the year and some of the changes that occur from one season to the next.
- Ask the children to look for signs of the changing seasons as you reread the story. *Which season does the book start with? How do you know which season is which?*
- Have the children work in groups creating collages for each of the seasons.

Then the river turned to ice. It was winter.

After a long time the ice began to melt. The sun shone and flowers began to bloom.

Talking about time

Sequencing in words and pictures

- Brainstorm and list the story's main events.

- Have the children work in pairs to illustrate each event.

- Sequence the children's illustrations on a long chart.

- Add time-phrases from the story, such as "at last", to make a "language timeline" for the pictures.

- Write the story's main events on cards. The children can take turns sequencing these on the chart to retell the story.

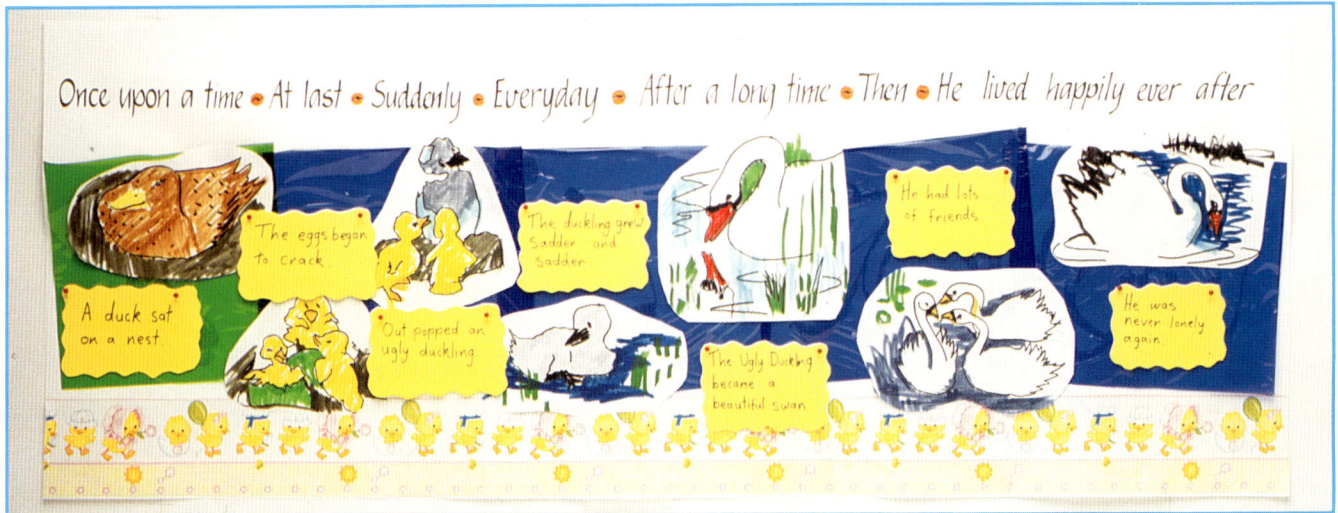

Once upon a time • At last • Suddenly • Everyday • After a long time • Then • He lived happily ever after

A duck sat on a nest

The eggs began to crack.

Out popped an ugly duckling

The duckling grew sadder and sadder.

The Ugly Duckling became a beautiful swan

He had lots of friends.

He was never lonely again.

Making a rebus story

Visual thinking

- Discuss how some of the words in the story might be replaced with pictures.

- Have the children work in pairs to retell events from the story in this way.

- Share and discuss, then bind the children's rebus episodes to form a book.

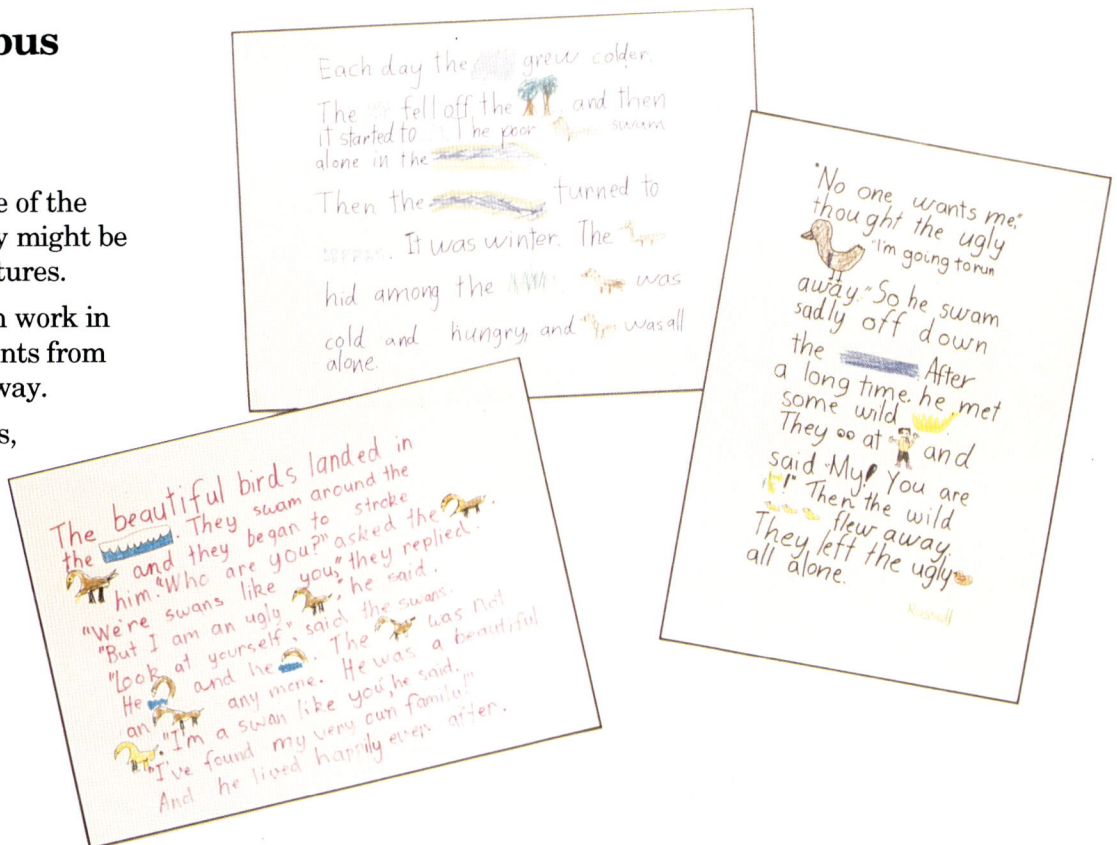

Each day the ■ grew colder. The ■ fell off the ■ and then it started to ■. The poor ■ swam alone in the ■.
Then the ■ turned to ■. It was winter. The ■ hid among the ■. ■ was cold and hungry and ■ was all alone.

The beautiful birds landed in the ■. They swam around the ■ and they began to stroke him. "Who are you?" asked the ■. "We're swans like you," they replied. "But I am an ugly ■," said the ■. "Look at yourself," said the swans. He ■ and he ■. He was a beautiful ■ any more. He was a swan like you," he said. an ■. "I'm a swan like you," he said. "I've found my very own family." And ■ he lived happily ever after.

"No one wants me," thought the ugly ■. "I'm going to run away." So he swam sadly off down the ■. After a long time he met some wild ■. They ■ at ■ and said "My! You are ■!" Then the wild ■ flew away. They left the ugly ■ all alone.

Other sad characters

Comparing characters and emotions

- As a class, discuss why the Ugly Duckling was sad.

- Brainstorm other stories in which characters are sad. *Why are they sad? Do they become happier?*

- The children can select sad characters and draw and describe them.

- As a follow-up, ask the children what makes them sad; they may wish to write about and illustrate their responses.

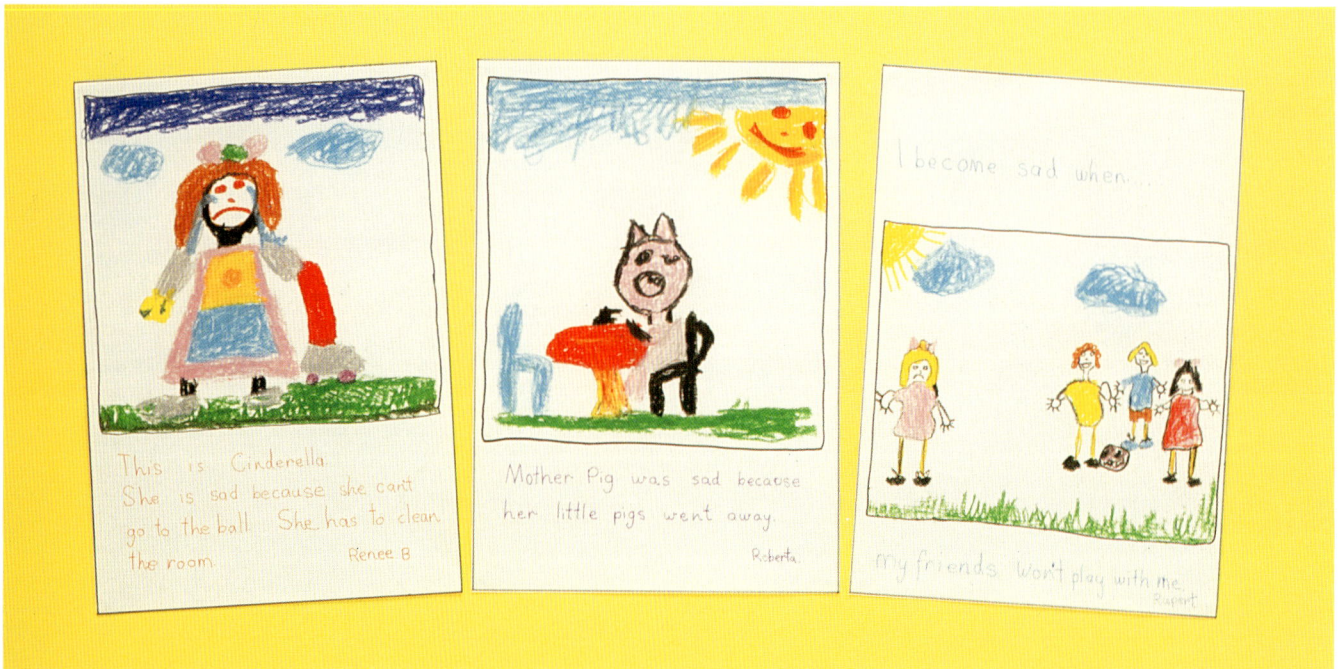

- Share and display.

This is Cinderella. She is sad because she can't go to the ball. She has to clean the room. Renee B

Mother Pig was sad because her little pigs went away. Roberta

I become sad when... my friends won't play with me. Rupert

Some good advice

Language

- Ask the children to put themselves in the place of the Ugly Duckling. *How would you have reacted? What would you have done?*

- Give each child a copy of Blackline Master 11, and have them write the advice they would give the Ugly Duckling.

- Have them illustrate their advice.

- Share and display.

Where do birds go?

Science: research

- Discuss what the class has learned about ducks from reading the story. Record this information on a list.

- Make a list of the questions the class might have about ducks, such as why they have webbed feet or where they go in winter. This list could be expanded to cover all birds.

- The children can select one of these questions and explore it further.

In Winter, geese fly to where it is warm.

by Christine

Making swans

Art

- Collect thin cardboard, paste, newspapers, stapler and cotton wool. Then show the children how they can make swans by:

  — drawing and cutting out two swan shapes and stapling them together, leaving a gap in the back;

  — stuffing crumpled newspapers into the swan and stapling it shut;

  — decorating by painting, or by pasting on cotton wool.

How did the egg get into the nest?

Problem solving: exploring different solutions

- *How did the swan's egg get into the duck's nest?* As a class, list some possibilities.

- The children can select an idea and write about it. These can be illustrated and shared.

- Display the work, adding more ideas over time.

- To follow up, the children can vote for the best solution, and tally and graph the votes.

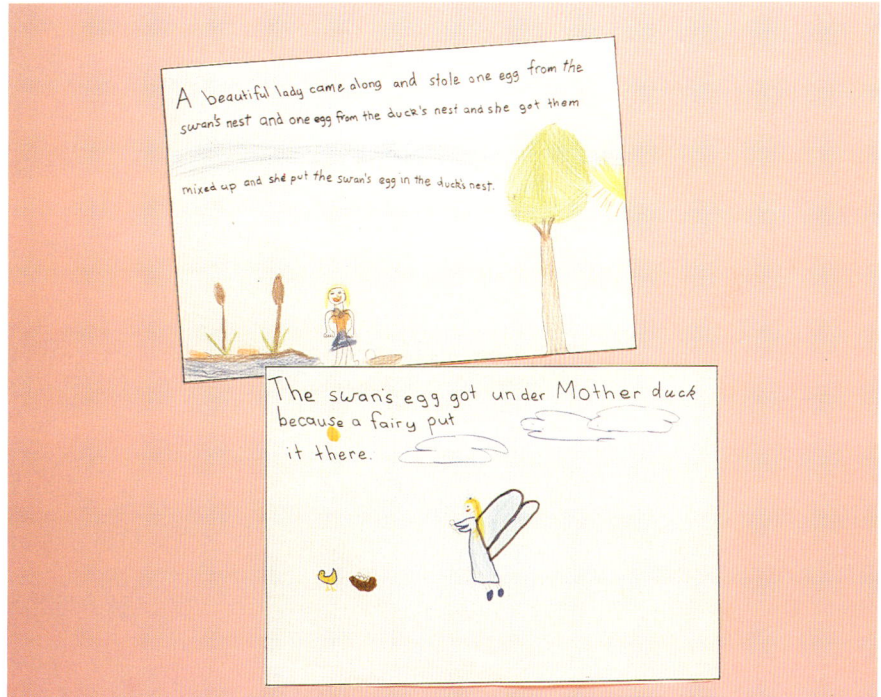

A beautiful lady came along and stole one egg from the swan's nest and one egg from the duck's nest and she get them mixed up and she put the swan's egg in the duck's nest.

The swan's egg got under Mother duck because a fairy put it there.

Why Frog and Snake Can't Be Friends

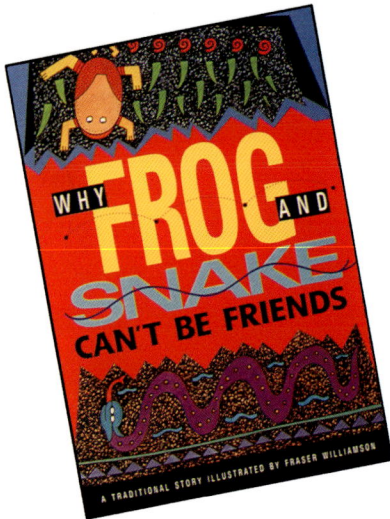

Why Frog and Snake Can't Be Friends uses a gently humorous style and repetitive structure to contrast and explain the innocent antics of a frog and a snake. The story leads into the exploration of character and relationships, as well as the operation of food chains.

Making jumping frogs

Art and mathematics (measuring and graphing)

Note: Have some fun — make your own frog before helping the children to make theirs.

- Give each child a piece of thin card about 8 cm × 14 cm.

- Demonstrate the steps on Blackline Master 12 one at a time, and have the children follow you.

- The children can name and label their completed frogs.

- Press lightly on the frogs' tails to make them leap. The children can hold a jumping contest, recording and graphing the distance each frog jumps.

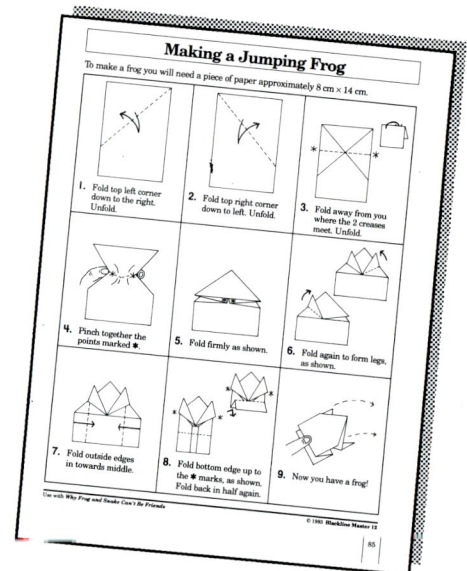

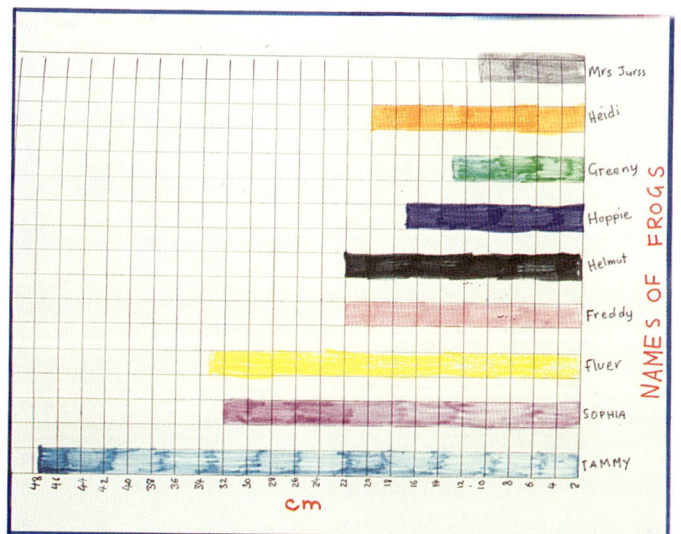

Food web

Science

- Brainstorm a list of creatures that snakes eat.

- Each child can select and illustrate a different creature from the snakes' food web.

- Arrange these on a chart and connect with arrows. Share and display.

- *Which of the animals eaten by snakes also eat each other? Use a different coloured marker to draw arrows between these.*

- As a follow-up activity, have the children suggest ways of grouping the animals on the chart; for example, by colour, size, body covering, number of legs or whether they lay eggs.

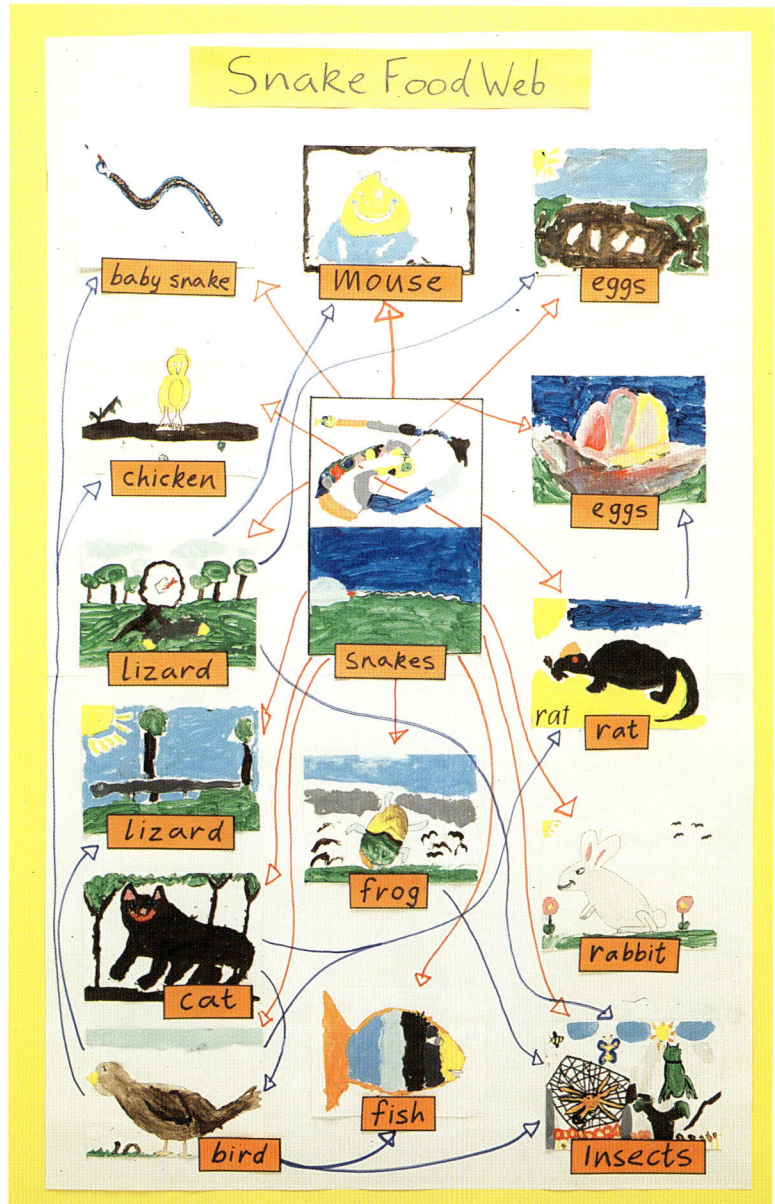

Making snakes

Art

- Make snakes by crumpling newspapers into old stockings. Decorate the snakes with fabric scraps.

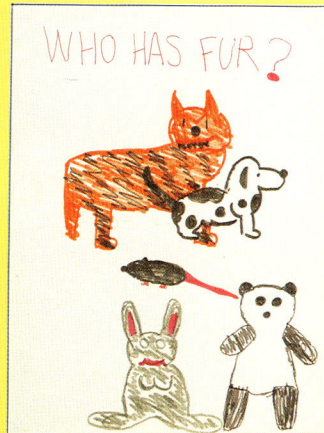

Putting on a puppet play

Language, drama and art

- Cut frog and snake shapes out of thin card. The children can colour them, and decorate with cotton wool, buttons and pipe cleaners. (Note: sock puppets make good snakes as well.)

- Make stick puppets by attaching craft sticks to each shape.

- Make a puppet stage by cutting a window in a large cardboard box, or by turning a table on its side for the actors to crouch behind.

- The children can prepare written invitations and invite other classes or teachers to their performance.

Dear Mr Bowham,
we are putting on
a play. It is called
why frog and snake
can't be friends.
We would like to
invite all of 2e to
watch our play.

Measuring in snake lengths

Mathematics (measurement of length)

- Cut out a strip of paper 1 m × 8 cm for each child. The children can draw a snake on their paper, and decorate it.

- Review how to measure by repeated use of one unit. The children can then measure various parts of the school, such as the classroom or a section of playground, in "snake lengths".

- Share and compare the children's results.

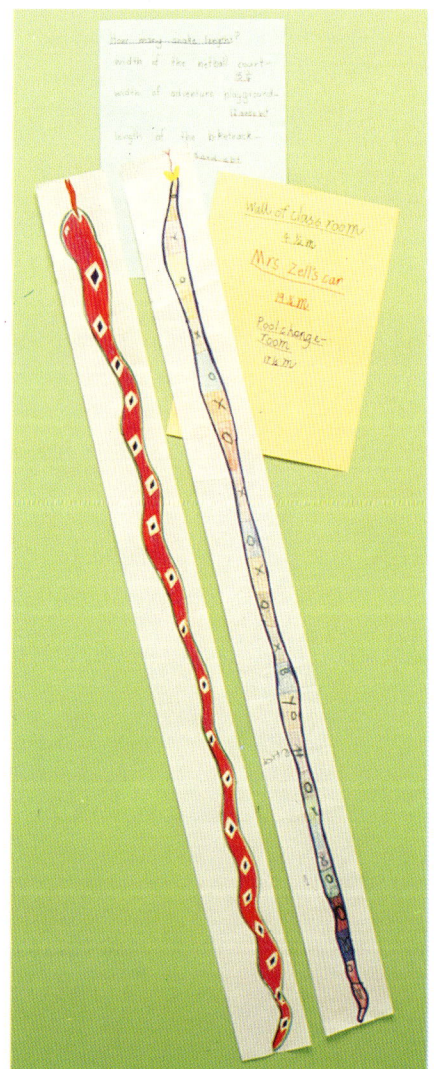

Making a character chart

Using descriptive language

- Brainstorm words that describe Snakeson.

- Write the words describing Snakeson around the edge of a chart. In the middle, draw a snake shape for the children to decorate with fabric scraps.

- Display the chart.

- Do the same for Frogchild.

- Compare Frogchild and Snakeson's similarities and differences; brainstorm why they could/couldn't become friends.

- Compile this information on a chart of *Similarities and Differences*.

- As a follow-up activity, the children could write about How Frog and Snake *Could Be Friends*, or explain the lack of friendship between other creatures, such as spiders and flies or cats and mice.

SNAKESON
Slick, lithe and slithery
active
playful
happy
obedient
pretty
helpful
cuddly
nice
friend
loving
sne

FROGCHILD
friendly
playful
truthful
lovely
trustworthy
Helpful
happy
kind
fun
honest
funny
hip
quick

Investigating patterns in nature

Science and mathematics

- Collect photographs of snakes. Compare and discuss their skin patterns. *How are they similar? Do the patterns serve any purpose?*

- *What other patterns are there in nature?* Look for examples of symmetry (butterfly wings, leaf veins) and geometrical shapes (honeycomb is hexagonal; and if you draw a line connecting the tips of some flowers, the petals form a pentagon).

- The children can describe and draw one of the patterns they have found.

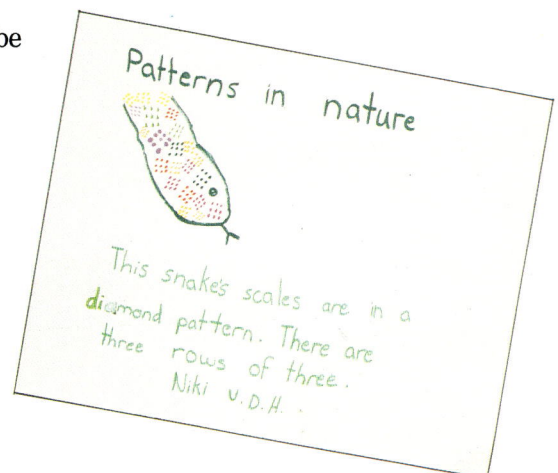

Patterns in nature

This snake's scales are in a diamond pattern. There are three rows of three. Niki V.D.H.

The Musicians of Bremen

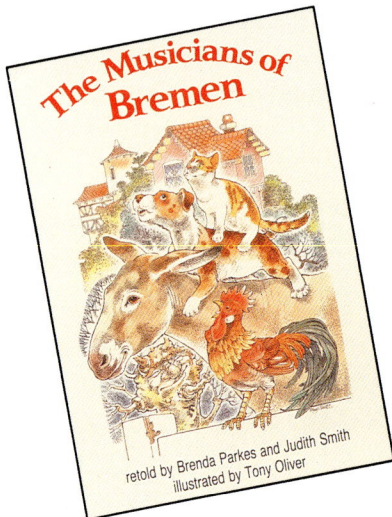

retold by Brenda Parkes and Judith Smith
illustrated by Tony Oliver

The Musicians of Bremen is an endearing story of triumph over adversity, as a group of old unwanted animals band together to support each other and find new dignity when they rid Bremen of robbers. Reader responses through mapping, music, mathematics and language stem naturally from this old tale.

Drawing a map

Art and visual thinking

- Discuss the animals' journey, where they stop and what happens to them.

- The children can draw maps of the journey showing, for example, the animals' original homes, the robbers' house and Bremen.

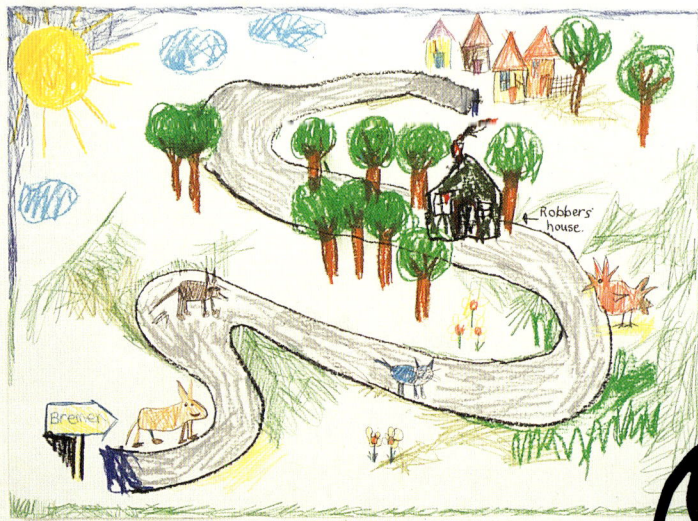

Animal antics

A discussion activity

- Make cut-outs of the animals in the story. (These can be re-used later for the shadow play; see page 68.)

- Display an animal shape on an overhead projector. Ask the children to tell what they know about the animal, both from the story and from real life.

- As a follow-up, have the children close their eyes and select an animal shape; they can then describe it by feel and try to tell which animal it is.

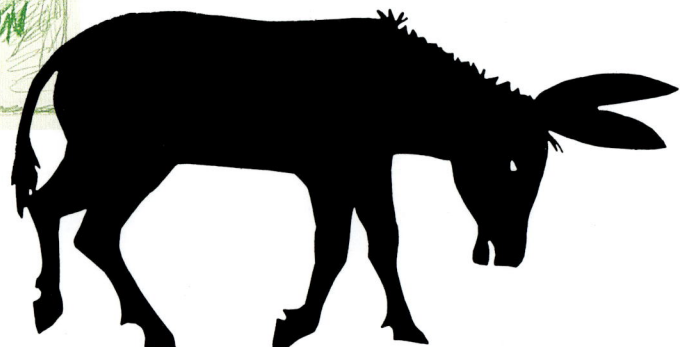

Animal facts

Language and science

- Select one of the animals and write its name on the board.
- Brainstorm information about that animal; what it did, what it looked like and its role in the story.
- Draw arrows radiating to each piece of information; then link related items, such as legs and hooves.
- The children can work in groups to record similar information about the other animals in the story.
- Discuss the differences and similarities between the animals.
- As a follow-up, the children can keep an on-going list of animal questions that they would like to research.

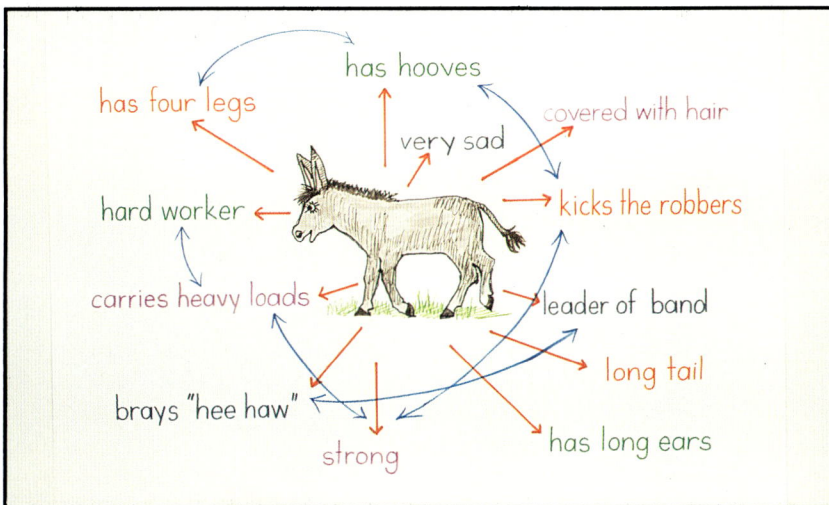

has hooves
has four legs
covered with hair
very sad
hard worker
kicks the robbers
carries heavy loads
leader of band
long tail
brays "hee haw"
has long ears
strong

DONKEYS
Why do donkeys have long ears?
What is a group of donkeys called?
How long do donkeys live?
Can you ride donkeys?
What are baby donkeys called?

What's that sound?

Social studies (classifying sounds)

- Talk about the sounds in the story — musical and animal.
- Take the children for a walk around the school; have them list the sounds they hear.
- Discuss how they could group the sounds; for example, people, traffic or animal sounds.
- The children can work in pairs to illustrate and describe a group of sounds.
- To follow up, the children can write statements and questions as a basis for further research on sound.

Traffic
beep
bells ring
WALK
tyres screeching

School
children talking laughing
Teacher talking
bell ringing
feet running

Putting on a shadow play

Drama

- The children can make shadow puppets by cutting animal shapes from strong card and attaching cardboard or wooden handles to them.

- Have the actors hide behind an overturned table, and use a sheet as a screen. Position a light to shine from behind the actors.

- The children can create music to accompany the play, and invite other classes to watch the performance.

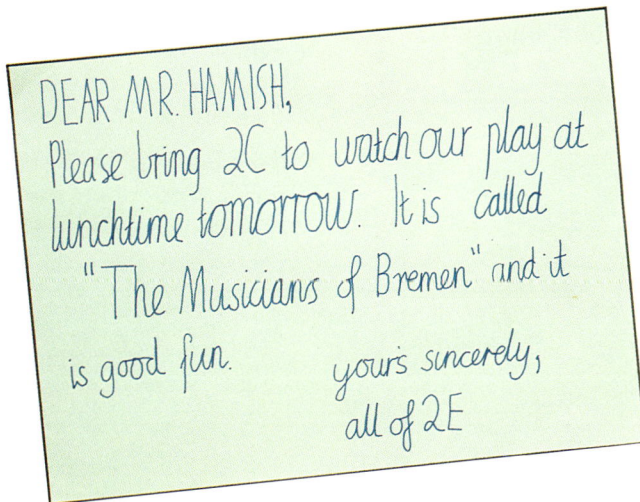

DEAR MR. HAMISH,
Please bring 2C to watch our play at lunchtime tomorrow. It is called "The Musicians of Bremen" and it is good fun.
yours sincerely,
all of 2E

Creating posters

Language

- Brainstorm ideas for posters related to the story. Here are some possibilities:
  — a bravery award for the animals from the city of Bremen.
  — a program for the animals' first concert.
  — a poster for a Musicians of Bremen rock band.
  — a poster advertising the class performance of *The Musicians of Bremen*.

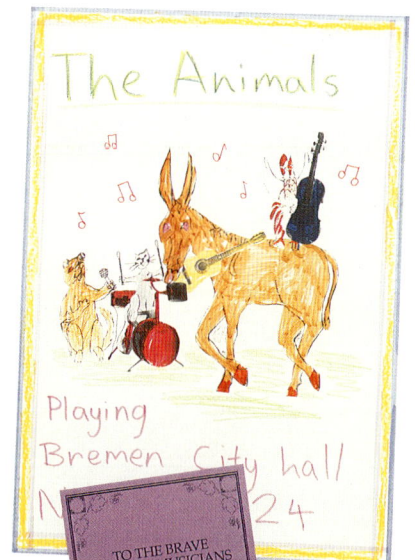

The Animals
Playing
Bremen City hall
24

TO THE BRAVE
BREMEN MUSICIANS

With grateful thanks
from
the people
of
Bremenstown

Work wanted

Exploring language through advertisements

- Collect samples of Work Wanted advertisements and share them with the children.

- Discuss the information provided. *How was it written?*

- As a class, select an animal from the story and write a Work Wanted advertisement for it.

- The children can then use Blackline Master 13 to write an advertisement for each animal. Share and display.

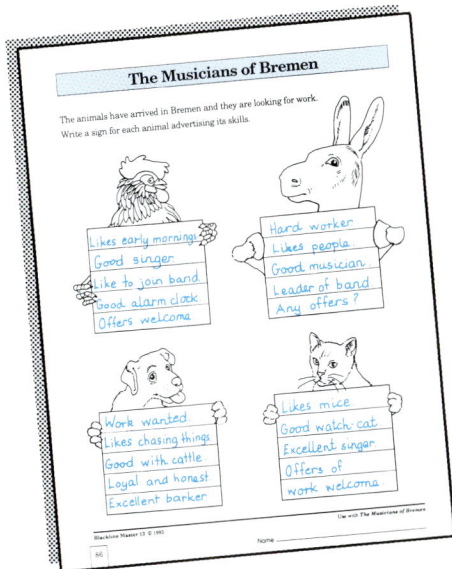

In memoriam

Art and social studies

- Collect and display pictures of statues; discuss why statues are built and what might be written on them.

- Collect playdough, clay and plasticine; the children can design and make statues of the story's characters and write captions to go with them.

- Alternatively, the children can design and draw statues.

Other suggestions

- Write a letter from one of the robbers giving his explanation of what happened after the robbery.

- Select an animal from the story and write a Lost Animal notice.

- Find and share other stories about clever animals.

Why Flies Buzz

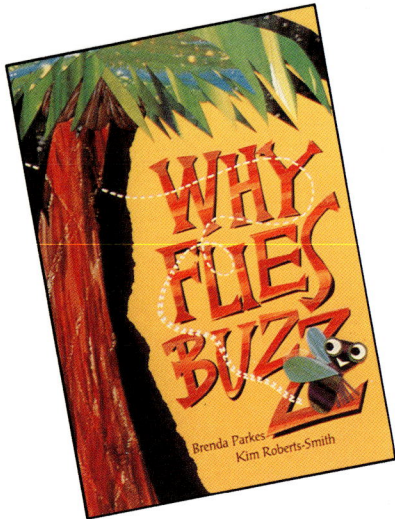

Why Flies Buzz is a lively story with a great deal of humour built into its repetitive structure. Reader responses to the story could include a range of art and drama activities, as well as related science and social studies investigations.

Recreating a scene

Sharing responses

- Provide an assortment of collage materials.

- Have the children choose a scene from the book and use the materials to illustrate it.

- The children can write the speech for each scene on detachable cardboard "speech bubbles".

- Display the collages and encourage the children to vary the speech bubbles each day. For example, they might create new speech bubbles using rebus words, colloquial language or a language the class is studying.

How to make a sundial

Science and procedural text

- Discuss sundials and how they are used.

- The children can work in pairs to make a sundial. Each pair will need a paper cup, a large piece of paper, a pencil and a piece of plasticine.

- Poke a hole in the bottom of the cup and push the pencil through it.

- Fix the cup to the paper with plasticine and place in the sun.

- Mark the paper at the shadow line each hour and record the time.

- Have the children write "how-to" instructions to explain how they made their sundials.

- As a follow-up, investigate solar power and how it is used.

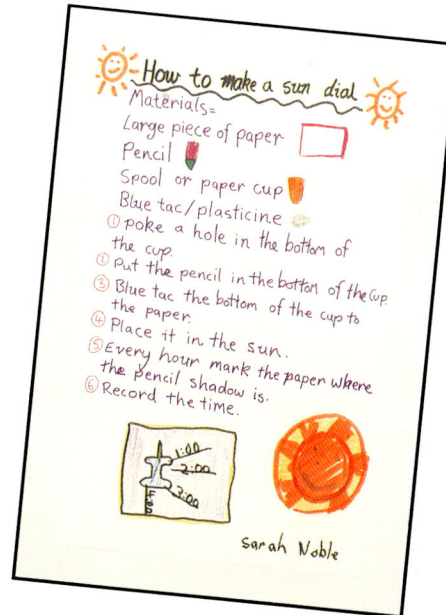

Finding out about the sun

Science: research

- List facts the children know about the sun.

- Leave the list open, researching and adding more information over several days.

- Make up a class book of sun facts.

- Share and display.

How people and animals communicate

Science and social studies

- Discuss and research questions such as, *How do people communicate? Is this different from how animals communicate?*

- The children can make charts to show the various methods of communication.

- Compare the charts and discuss the advantages and disadvantages of different forms of communication.

Making the Great Spirit and the fly

Art and drama

- The children can make flies by attaching cellophane or crepe paper "wings" to sections of egg cartons.

- The children can make the Great Spirit mask by decorating paper bags and attaching crepe paper streamers for arms.

- Use the flies and masks as props in retelling the story.

- To follow up, the children can write "how-to" instructions for the flies and masks.

Write to the author and illustrator

Exploring and explaining responses

- Discuss the book with the children. Ask questions such as, *Which animal did you like most? Which part of the book was the funniest? What did you think the book would be about?*

- The children can write to the author and/or illustrator telling them what they thought of the story.

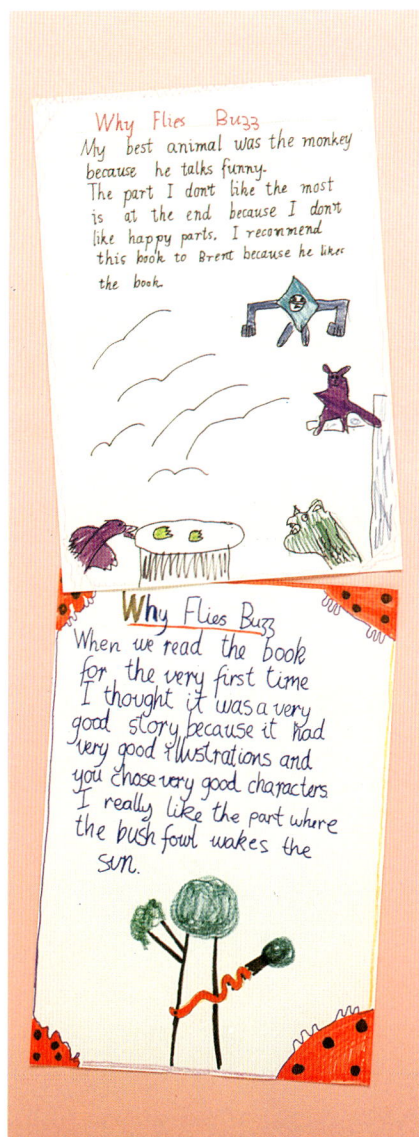

If only...

Problem solving: cause and effect

- Talk about how one event in the book leads to another. List the chain of events on the chalkboard.

- *What might have happened if one event hadn't taken place?* Brainstorm other possible outcomes.

- Give each of the children a large piece of paper and have them fold it into six squares. They can write a story with six events that follow each other in a chain, using one square for each event.

- The children can cut their stories into six parts, place the pieces in a paper bag and then give them to a partner for sequencing.

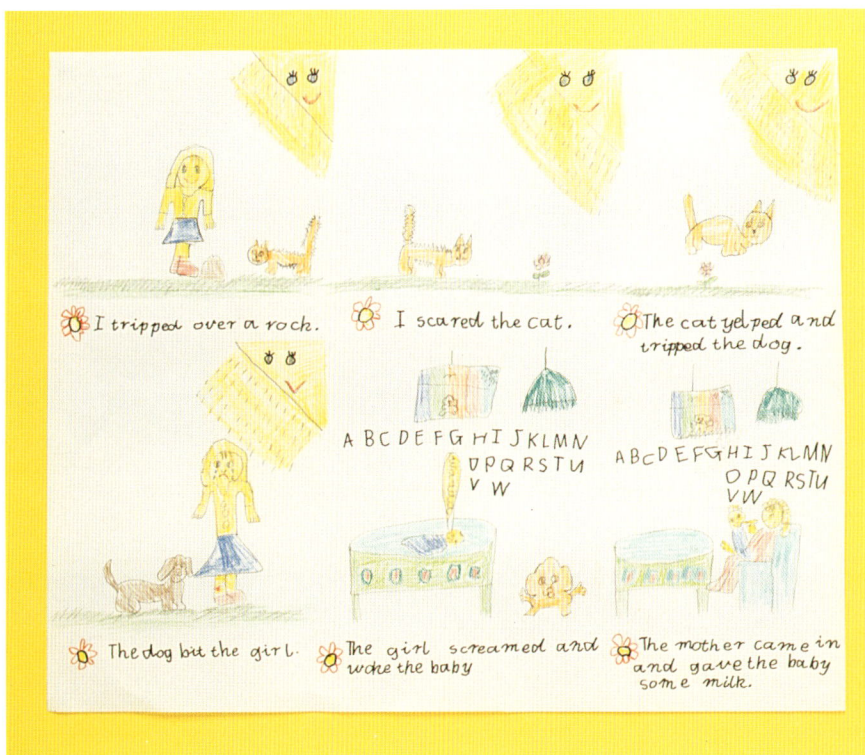

Other suggestions

- Read some poems about the sun; the children can then write and illustrate their own sun poems.

- Investigate different sun legends. The children can then write and compile their own sun legends.

- *What would happen if there were no sun?* The children can suggest some possibilities, then select a topic to research.

What Comes Next?

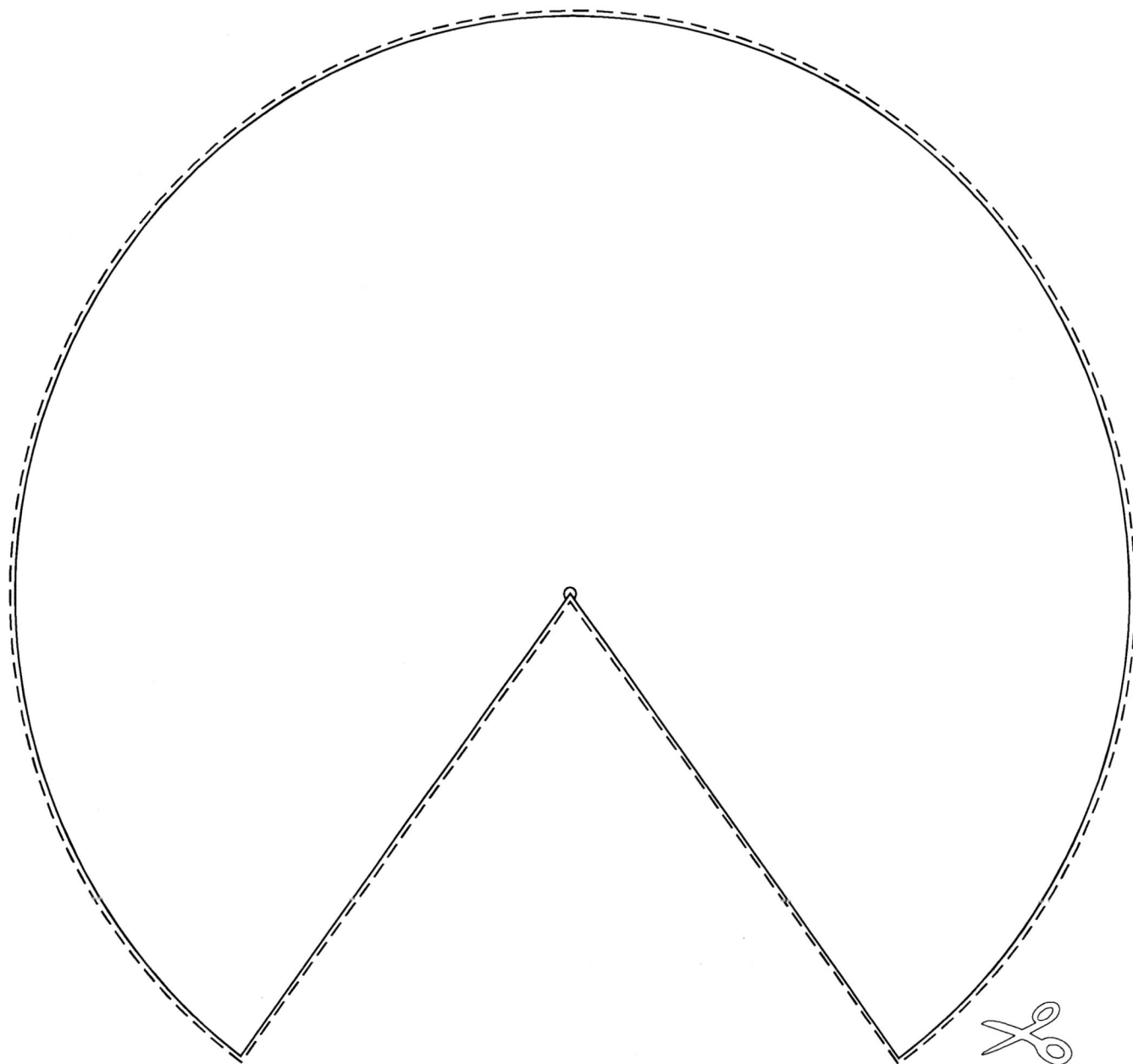

What Comes Next?

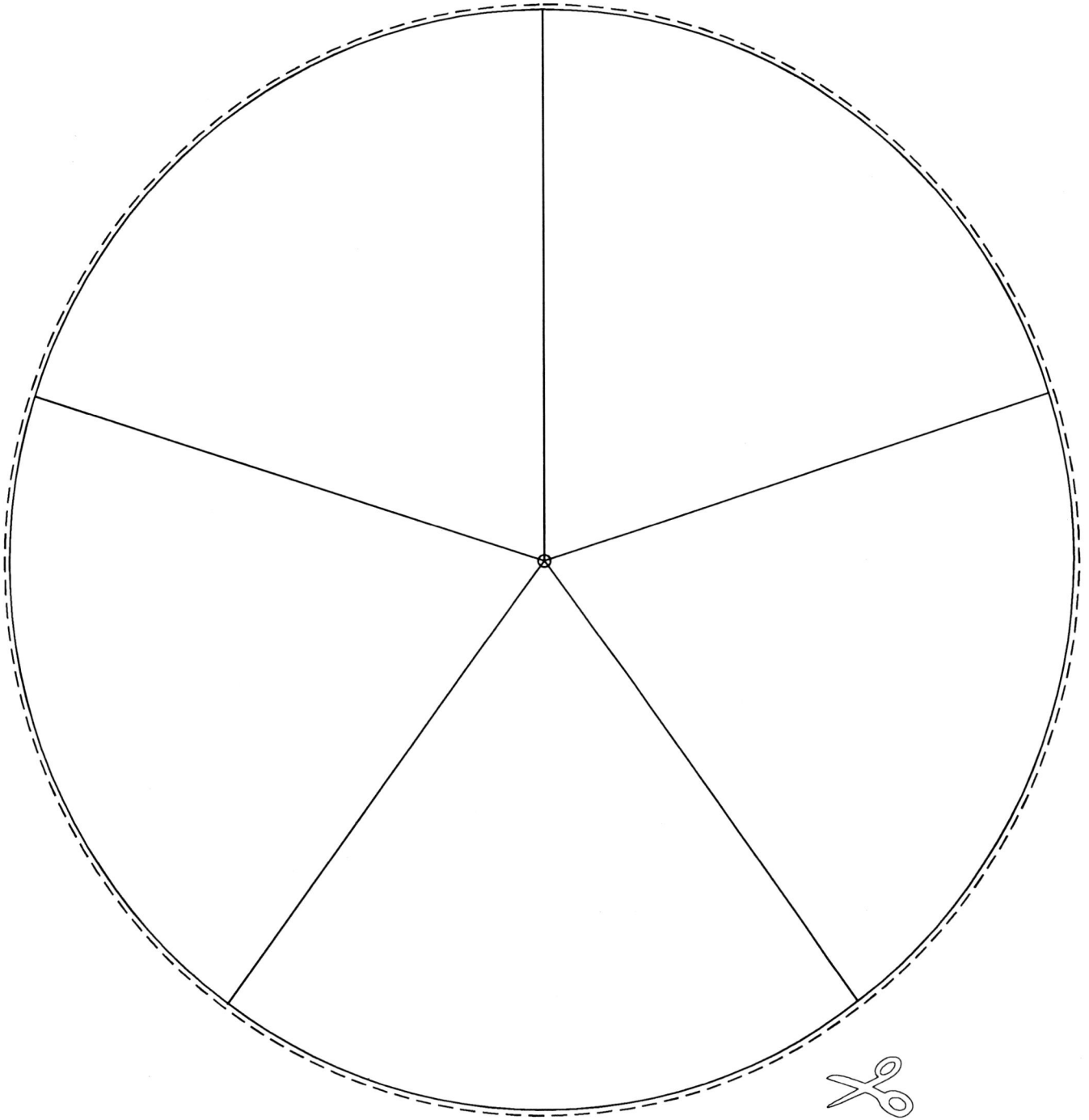

Then What Happened?

Look at the pictures. Write what you think the Gingerbread Man is saying.
Then draw two more pictures to show what might happen next.

1	2
3	4
5	6

Use with *The Gingerbread Man*

Name _____

My Plan to Catch a Pig, by B. B. Wolf.

Invent the wolf's plan to catch a pig.

Include at least three of the items pictured, plus one or two of your own choice.

Describe and draw your plan in the space below.

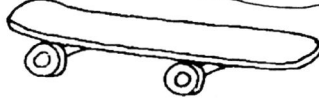

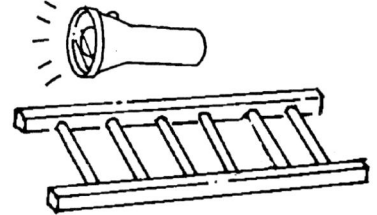

What Do You Think?

Find the parts of the story which match these pictures.

Then write what each of the characters might be thinking.

Use with *Goldilocks and the Three Bears*

Name _____

Some, More, Most

Some for me

More for me

Most for me

Big and Small

Cut out the lion and the mouse along the dotted lines.

Find things that are wider or narrower than the mouse.

Find things that are longer or shorter than the lion.

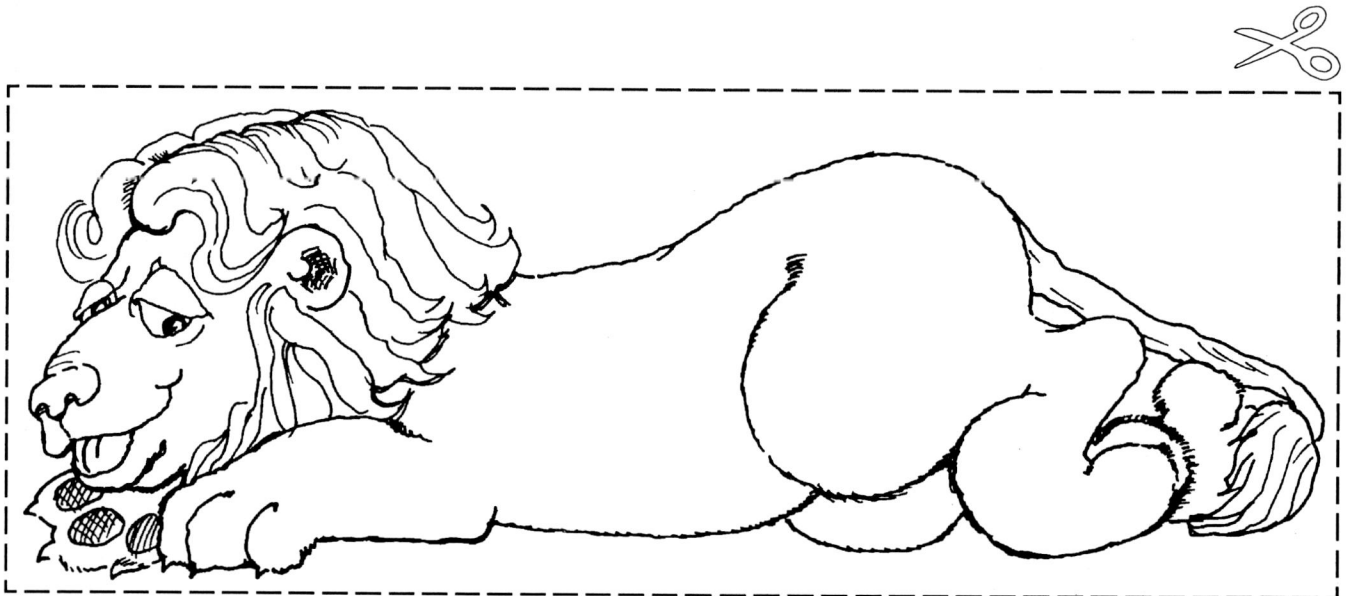

Find the Way

Find a path that Chicken Little can follow to reach the castle. Make sure that she visits all her friends on the way, without going past Foxy Loxy's den.

Read All About It

BRIDGE MYSTERY

Residents in the vicinity of Troll Bridge were woken last night by a loud splash . .

TROLL TAKES TUMBLE

Police have begun a hunt for the Three Billy Goats Gruff, who have been reported missing from their hillside . . .

GOATS MEET THEIR MATCH

Write the story of the Goats and the Troll for a newspaper.

Begin with a headline and opening sentence from above, or write your own.

_____

_____

_____

_____

_____

_____

_____

_____

_____

_____

_____

Name _____

Find the Words

This wonderword contains 20 words made up from Rumpelstiltskin's name.
Can you find them all?

A	E	S	K	I	N	P	L	U	M	P
P	E	T	I	L	E	S	I	O	T	U
A	B	I	L	P	U	T	K	N	I	T
M	E	L	T	C	D	R	E	F	L	G
L	H	T	I	N	J	U	S	K	E	L
I	M	S	T	I	R	S	K	I	L	L
M	P	R	U	N	E	T	N	O	P	Q
P	R	I	N	T	S	T	E	P	S	R

SKIN	STEPS	PET	TILE
STILTS	KNIT	MELT	PUT
PLUM	LIMP	KILT	PRUNE
LUMP	SKILL	LIKES	IN
TIN	PRINT	RUST	STIR

Name _____

Some Good Advice

Dear Friend,
The other ducks don't want to be
my friends. This makes me unhappy.
What do you think I should do?

Yours sincerely,

The Duckling.

The Ugly Duckling has written asking for your advice. What will you tell him?

_____

_____

_____

_____

_____

_____

_____

_____

Making a Jumping Frog

To make a frog you will need a piece of paper approximately 8 cm × 14 cm.

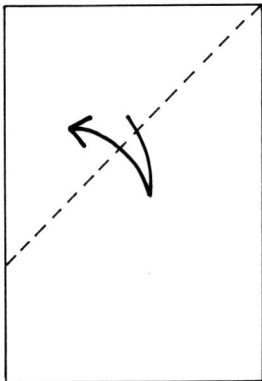

1. Fold top left corner down to the right. Unfold.

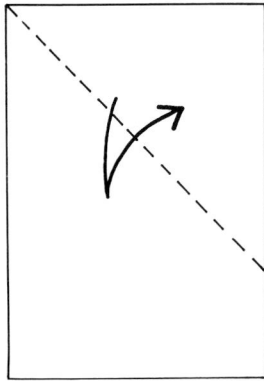

2. Fold top right corner down to left. Unfold.

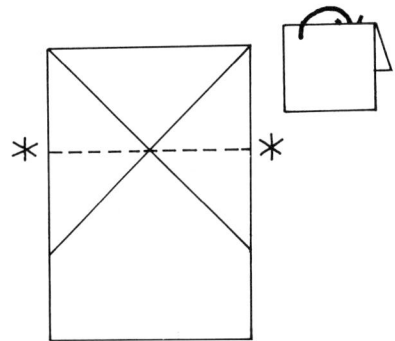

3. Fold away from you where the 2 creases meet. Unfold.

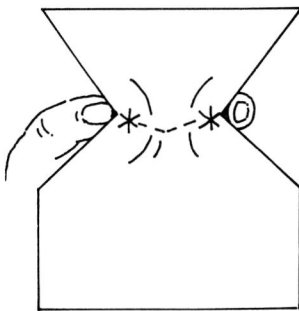

4. Pinch together the points marked ✱.

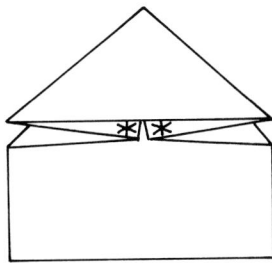

5. Fold firmly as shown.

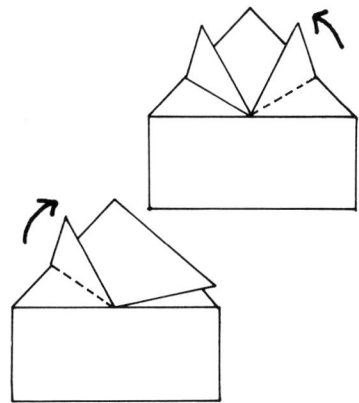

6. Fold again to form legs, as shown.

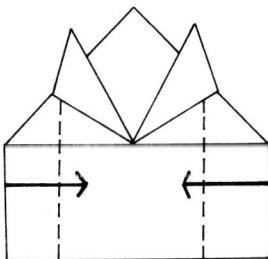

7. Fold outside edges in towards middle.

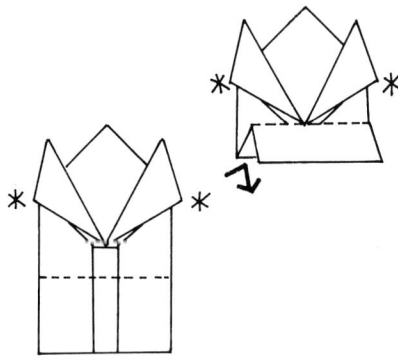

8. Fold bottom edge up to the ✱ marks, as shown. Fold back in half again.

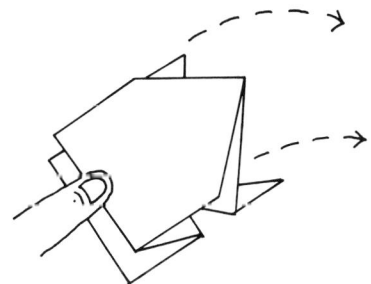

9. Now you have a frog!

© 1993 **Blackline Master 12**

The Musicians of Bremen

The animals have arrived in Bremen and they are looking for work.
Write a sign for each animal advertising its skills.

Who Am I?

Think of a character from a story your class has read.

Write a clue about your character using one of the sentence starters below.

Ask a partner to guess the answer. If he or she can't guess, write another clue.

Clues

I like to eat _____

I don't like _____

My friends are _____

I live _____

My hair is _____

I am very _____

My age is _____

Some of the things I do are _____

_____

_____

Write more clues below if needed.

Personality Profile for _____

Draw a story character in the picture frame.

In each oval, write something that character does in the story.

In each triangle, write a word to describe the character.

Draw a line from each oval to its matching triangle.

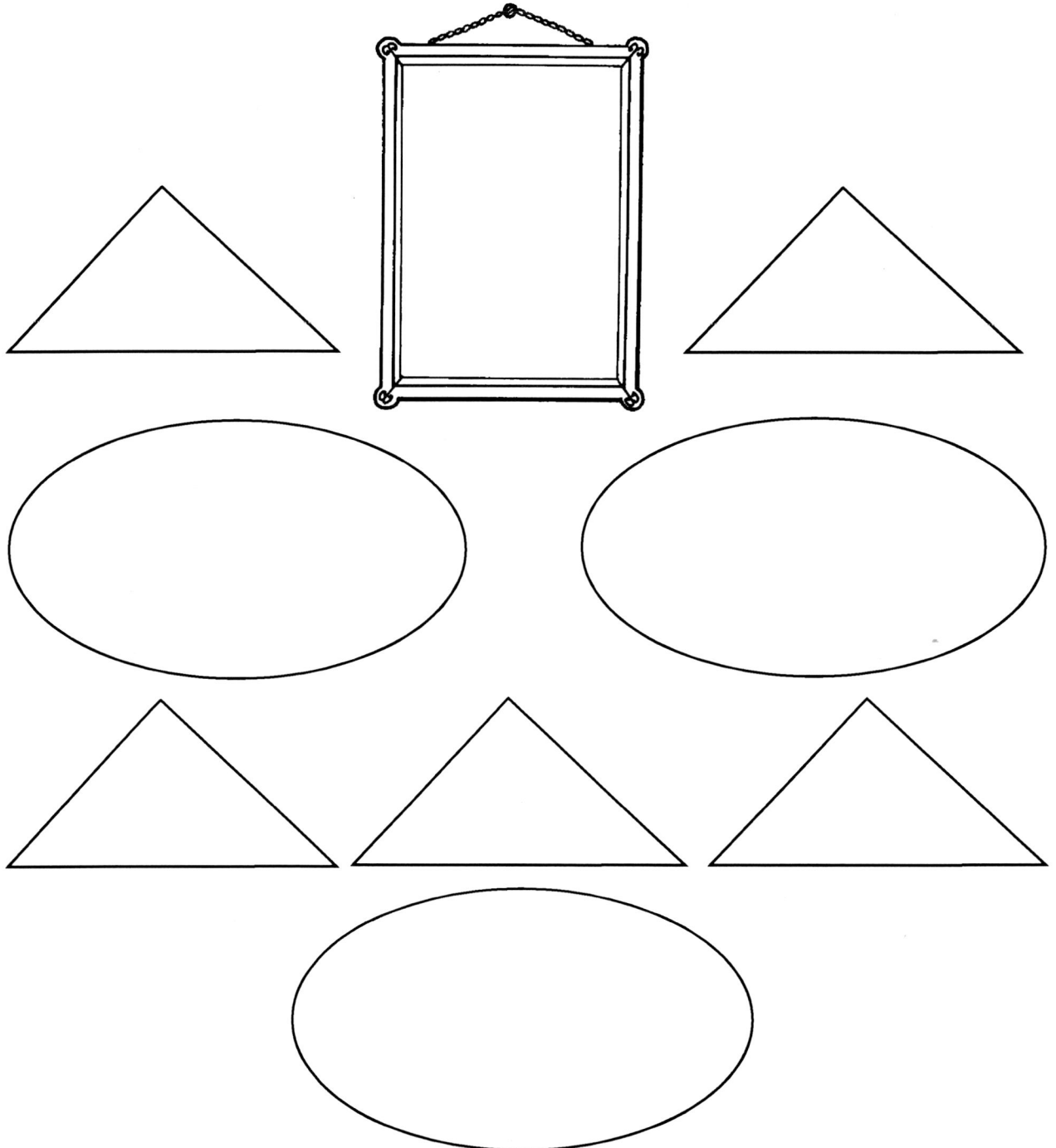

Compare the Characters

Select two story characters.

Shade in the graph below to show what you think each character is like.

Character's name _____

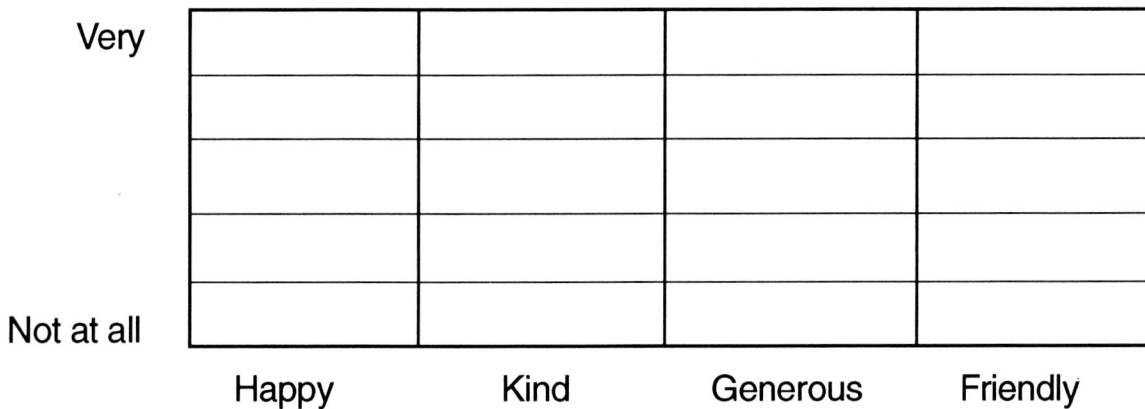

Very

Not at all

      Happy   Kind   Generous   Friendly

Character's name _____

Very

Not at all

      Happy   Kind   Generous   Friendly

Compare the graphs. Are the two characters similar or different? Tell why.

_____

_____

_____

Use with any story   © 1993 **Blackline Master 16**

Name _____

Do-it-yourself Dough

What you need:

- $\frac{3}{4}$ cup flour
- $\frac{1}{2}$ cup cornflour
- $\frac{1}{2}$ cup salt

- bowl
- about $\frac{1}{2}$ cup warm water

Method:

1. Mix all ingredients in the bowl.
2. Gradually add warm water to make a thick dough.
3. Dust with flour to reduce stickiness.
4. Roll out to even thickness.
5. Mould or cut out shapes of your choice.
6. Leave to dry for two or three days, then paint.

Draw what you made from the dough.

Write instructions so that a friend could make the same thing.

Bibliography

Traditional tales have been told and retold over hundreds of years, with different storytellers adding their own embellishments or adapting the tale for their own cultures. For example, there are four versions of *The Gingerbread Man* listed in this bibliography — American, Scandinavian, Scottish and English — and each one focuses on a different aspect of the story, providing four distinct and individual retellings.

Children enjoy reading and comparing different versions of traditional tales, and are quick to notice variations in the way characters and events are described and depicted. This short bibliography provides a starting point for such comparisons.

The Little Red Hen

Galdone, P. 1985, *The Little Red Hen,* Clarion, New York.

A cat, a dog, a mouse and a hen all live together, but the hen does all the work. Every time she asks for help, the others refuse — until she makes a cake, when everybody offers to help her eat it.

Root, B., Nichols, R. & Oliver, D. 1975, *The Little Red Hen,* Macdonald & Co., London.

This book retells the traditional British folk tale in pictures and easy-to-read text. In this version, a cat, a duck and a pig are too busy to help the Little Red Hen plant, harvest or take the wheat to the mill. When she bakes bread, she shares it with her family instead of with these other animals.

Zemach, M. 1983, *The Little Red Hen,* Farrar, Strauss & Giroux.

A goose, a cat and a pig are too lazy to help the hen, but when she makes bread they offer to help her eat it.

The Gingerbread Man

Arbuthnot, M. H., "The Gingerbread Boy", in Arbuthnot, M. H., (compiler) 1961, *Time for Fairy Tales,* Scott, Foresman & Co., Illinois.

In this American version, which appeared in St Nicholas Magazine in May 1875, a little old man and woman want a son. They bake a son out of gingerbread, but he runs away when the oven is opened, and is eaten by a fox.

Arbuthnot, M.H. "The Pancake", in *Arbuthnot, M.H.* 1961.

In this Scandinavian version of the story, a mother makes a pancake to feed her seven hungry children. Not wanting to be eaten, the pancake runs away. It is eaten by a pig that tricks the pancake into crossing a river on its snout.

Ireson, B. 1962, *The Gingerbread Man,* Faber & Faber Ltd, London.

A gingerbread man escapes when the oven is opened. He is chased by the woman who made him and others who see them running by, and eaten by a fox who tricks him into crossing a river on his back.

Wilson, B.K., "The Fox and the Little Bannock", in Wilson, B.K. 1954, *Scottish Folk Tales and Legends,* Oxford University Press, London.

In this Scottish version, a wife bakes three bannocks for her husband's supper. The smallest bannock doesn't want to be eaten and runs away, only to be eaten by a fox while crossing a river.

The Fox and the Little Red Hen

Green, H.J., "The Fox and the Little Red Hen", in Green H.J. 1930, *The Victorian Readers,* Government Printer, Melbourne.

The sly Fox and his mother plan to eat Little Red Hen for their supper. Their plan fails when Fox falls asleep and the hen escapes, leaving a heavy stone in her place.

The Three Little Pigs

Acosta, K. (illus.) 1977, *The Three Little Pigs,* Chatto & Windus, London.

This "peep-show" book is an adaptation of the traditional tale. In this version each little pig escapes and runs to the house of his brother. Finally, the three little pigs cook and eat the wolf.

Ross, T. 1983, *The Three Pigs,* Puffin, Melbourne.

In this contemporary version, the pigs escape their crowded city apartment and move to the country — only to be pursued by a modern day wolf.

Scieszka, J. 1991, *The Three Pigs,* Puffin, Melbourne.

When Mr A. Wolf bakes a cake for his grandmother, he starts a chain of events which shed new light on this old story.

Stobbs, W. 1965, *The Story of the Three Little Pigs,* The Bodley Head, London.

The text for this book was taken from J. O. Halliwell's version, printed in about 1860 — the earliest known printed English version. The first two pigs build their homes from straw, and are eaten; the third brother builds a brick house, and outwits and eats the wolf.

Goldilocks and the Three Bears

Galdone, P. 1972, *The Three Bears,* Clarion Books, New York.

Goldilocks visits the three bears' house while they are out. She tastes their porridge, tries their chairs and sleeps in wee bear's bed. She is scared off when the three bears come home and is never seen again.

Stobbs, W. 1964, *The Story of the Three Bears,* The Bodley Head, London.

In Robert Southey's original story, the visitor was a wicked old woman. In later versions she became Little Silver Hair. This picture book version by Stobbs follows the familiar retelling involving a golden-haired girl who tries out the porridge and chairs before finally falling asleep in baby bear's bed.

The Lion and the Mouse

Jacobs, J., "The Lion and the Mouse", in Jacobs, J. 1984, *The Fables of Aesop,* Macmillan & Co., London.

A mouse is caught by a lion, and only released after promising that one day it will help the lion. When the lion is trapped, the mouse gnaws through the ropes that bind him.

Wildsmith, B. 1963, *The Lion and the Rat,* Oxford University Press, London.

In this version, a rat walking between the paws of a lion is caught, but set free when it promises to help the lion in time of need; it does this by gnawing through the net when the lion is trapped.

Chicken Little

Galdone, P. 1968, *Henny Penny,* World's Work, Windmill Press, Surrey. Also, 1975, William Clowes & Sons, London.

In this retelling, Paul Galdone gives some of the characters different names; the animals are ultimately eaten by Mr and Mrs Fox and their seven little foxes.

Stobbs, W. 1968, *Henny Penny,* The Bodley Head, London. Reprinted 1971.

In this picture book, Henny Penny thinks the sky is falling and leads the other farmyard animals, Cocky-locky, Ducky-daddles, Goosey-poosey and Turkey-lurkey, to tell the king. One by one the animals are lured away and eaten by Foxy-woxy.

The Three Billy Goats Gruff

Brown, M. 1957, *The Three Billy Goats Gruff,* Harcourt, New York.

This version keeps closely to the Norwegian original in the setting for the text and in the dynamic illustrations.

Galdone, P. 1973, *The Three Billy Goats Gruff,* World's Work, Surrey, England.

This retelling features illustrations with a variety of perspectives of the goats as they cross the bridge, and large, close-up pictures of the troll.

The Fisherman and His Wife

Adams, R., "The Fisherman and His Wife", in Adams, R. 1981, *Grimm's Fairy Tales,* Routledge & Kegan Paul, London.

A Fisherman catches a magic fish which grants his wife's wishes — until she wishes to be God-like.

Haviland, V., "The Old Woman and the Fish", in Haviland, V. 1966, *Favourite Fairy Tales Told in Sweden,* The Bodley Head, London.

This is a retelling from *Fairy Tales From the Swedish*, by Nils Gabriel Djurklou, translated by H.L. Braeksfad, 1901, Heinemann, London. A widow catches a magic fish that grants her three wishes. She wishes that her water buckets will fill themselves, that whatever she strikes will break off, and that whatever she pulls will grow long. However, her wishes go terribly wrong — the buckets fill with water and take themselves home, her legs break and her nose grows long.

Shub, E. 1978, *The Fisherman and His Wife,* Greenwillow, New York.

The use of progressively darker colours clearly express the magic fish's displeasure at the wife's continued demands.

Rumpelstiltskin

Leonie, B. 1955, *French Tales and Fairy Stories,* Oxford University Press, London.

A peasant girl bites holes in a pancake which a passing prince mistakes for lace. The girl is taken to the castle to make more lace on pain of death! She makes a bargain with a goblin, who disappears when she finds out his name.

Nathan, S. 1968, *Rumpelstiltskin,* Whitman Publishing Company, Wisconsin.

A miller tells the king his daughter can spin straw into gold. The king announces that if she can't, she will be killed. She promises her firstborn to Rumpelstiltskin if he will help her, but later prevents him from taking her child by finding out his name.

Reeves, J., "Tom Tit Tot", in Reeves, J. 1954, *English Fables and Fairy Stories,* Oxford University Press, London.

A mother tells the king that her daughter can spin five skeins of flax a day. When the daughter marries the king, she learns that she must spin for one month each year, or die; she makes a bargain with Tom Tit Tot who does the spinning for her. He disappears when she guesses his name.

Wilson, B.K., "Whippetty Stourie", in Wilson, B.K. 1954, *Scottish Folk Tales and Legends,* Oxford University Press, London.

In this humorous version the husband, who had been going to replace his wife or kill her if she didn't learn to spin, throws the spinning wheel away after meeting the strange Whippetty Stourie and her friends.

Jack and the Beanstalk

Biro, V. 1989, *Jack and the Beanstalk,* Oxford University Press, Melbourne.

This is a modern retelling which has been simplified for young readers. It features an italicised refrain.

Brychta, J. 1971, *Jack and the Beanstalk,* Franklin Watts, London.

In this story Jack returns to the giant's castle in disguise, first as an old woman, then as a gypsy.

Herring, Ann & Watanabe, Ryuhei, 1972, *Jack and the Beanstalk,* Gakken Co., Japan.

In this photographic retelling, Jack learns on his first visit to the giant's castle that the giant once stole everything from Jack's father. Jack kills the giant and retrieves his father's goods.

Stobbs, W. 1965, *Jack and the Beanstalk,* Constable Young, London.

In this version Jack climbs the beanstalk three times; first he takes a bag of gold, then the hen that lays golden eggs, then a harp. He is chased by the ogre, whom he kills by chopping down the beanstalk while the ogre is still on it. Jack, now rich because of the ogre's gold, marries a princess.

Puss-in-Boots

Galdone, P. 1976, *Puss-in-Boots,* Clarion, New York.

This dramatic retelling portrays a debonair Puss helping his young master to make his fortune through a series of clever tricks.

Wilkinson, B. 1968, *Puss in Boots or The Master Cat,* The Bodley Head, London.

A miller dies, leaving his possessions to his three sons — but all the youngest gets is a cat. The cat can speak, and helps his young master to marry the King's daughter and become the Marquis of Carabas.

The Ugly Duckling

Andersen, Hans Christian, 1965, *The Ugly Duckling,* Charles Scribner's Sons, New York.

This story is translated from the original Danish. A mother duck hatches a swan, which leaves the nest because it is not accepted.

Why Frog and Snake Can't Be Friends

Aardema, V. 1981, *Bringing the Rain to Kapiti Plain,* Dial, New York.

This retelling of a Kenyan tale tells how Ki-pat breaks a drought by shooting an eagle feather into a cloud.

Bryan, A. "Why Frog and Snake Never Play Together" in Bryan, A. *Beat the Story-Drum, Pum-Pum,* Macmillan.

After playing together happily, Frog and Snake discover that they are meant to be enemies.

The Musicians of Bremen

Figes, E. 1962, *The Musicians of Bremen,* S. Mohn Verlag, Gutersloh; also 1967, Blackie & Sons, London.

A donkey, a cat, a dog and a rooster set out to earn a living as musicians. In the process they frighten off a band of robbers and earn the gratitude of the people of Bremen.

Haviland, V. 1959, "The Musicians of Bremen", in Haviland, V. 1966, *Favourite Fairy Tales Told in Sweden,* The Bodley Head, London.

This retelling by Virginia Haviland closely follows the original Brothers Grimm story of the four unwanted animals who band together.

Why Flies Buzz

Aardema, V. 1978, *Why Mosquitos Buzz in People's Ears,* Dial Press, New York.

When Mother Owl fails to wake the sun as she usually does, King Lion calls a meeting of the jungle animals to discover the reason. The culprit is the mosquito, who has set off a series of events by telling the iguana a tall tale.

Index

About the author

Brenda Parkes is currently Senior
Lecturer in Literacy Education in the
Faculty of Education at Griffith
University, Brisbane, Australia.
Before this, she spent fifteen years
teaching at the early childhood and
primary levels in both New Zealand
and Australia.

Brenda has an insider's knowledge of
traditional tales; as well as writing a
number of books for young readers,
she has retold many traditional tales
in shared book format. She is
committed to helping teachers
discover the wealth of learning
experiences that traditional tales can
provide.

"I believe that traditional tales
provide one of the richest resources for
teachers. Their enduring themes,
predictable plots and memorable
language and characters hold great
appeal for young readers, and inspire
activities which range right across the
curriculum."